THE ANATOMY LESSON
and other stories

THE ANATOMY LESSON

and other stories by

EVAN S. CONNELL, JR.

Short Story Index Reprint Series

BOOKS FOR LIBRARIES PRESS
FREEPORT, NEW YORK

Grateful acknowledgment is made to *New World Writing III,
The Paris Review, The Western Review, Tomorrow, Flair,* and
American Mercury, in which some of these stories originally
appeared.

INTERNATIONAL STANDARD BOOK NUMBER:
0-8369-4132-2

LIBRARY OF CONGRESS CATALOG CARD NUMBER:
79-38719

PRINTED IN THE UNITED STATES OF AMERICA
BY
NEW WORLD BOOK MANUFACTURING CO., INC.
HALLANDALE, FLORIDA 33009

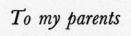

To my parents

Contents

The Anatomy Lesson   *3*

The Beau Monde of Mrs. Bridge   *25*

The Condor and the Guests   *45*

The Fisherman from Chihuahua   *55*

I'll Take You to Tennessee   *69*

The Walls of Ávila   *83*

I Came from Yonder Mountain   *113*

The Color of the World   *123*

The Trellis   *131*

Arcturus   *161*

The Yellow Raft   *209*

THE ANATOMY LESSON
and other stories

The Anatomy Lesson

North Fayer Hall stood on the final and lowest hill of the university, a little askew from the other buildings as if it were ashamed of its shabbiness and had turned partly away. Its window sills were pocked by cigarette burns and the doors of its green tin lockers had been pried open for so many years that few of them would lock any more; the creaking floors were streaked and spattered with drops of paint, dust lay upon the skylights, and because the ventilating system could not carry off so many fumes it seemed forever drenched in turpentine. Mercifully the little building was hidden each afternoon by the shadows of its huge, ivy-jacketed companions.

Just inside the front door was the office and studio of Professor A. B. Gidney, head of the art department, who taught ceramics, bookbinding, fashion design, and lettering. Professor Gidney's door was always open, even when he was teaching class somewhere else in the building, and in his studio were teacups and cookies and a hot plate which the students were free to use whenever they pleased. There was also a record player and a soft maple cabinet

containing albums of operettas and waltzes; every afternoon punctually at five the music started.

Behind his office were the student ateliers, each with
twenty or thirty short-legged chairs placed in a semicircle
around the model's platform, and at the extreme rear of
the building next to the fire escape, and reached by a dim
corridor which multiplied every footstep, stood the studio
of the other instructor.

This final studio was shaped like an up-ended coffin. In
the rafters which surrounded its skylight spiders were forever weaving, and because the window had not been
opened in years the air was as stale as that of an attic, always cold in December and always close in July. The
window as a matter of fact could not even be seen because
of the magazines and newspapers heaped atop a huge, iron-
bound trunk with a gibbous lid. In one corner of the room
a board rack held rows of somber oil paintings, each nearly
the same: marshes in the center of which one hooded figure was standing with head bowed. The first few strokes of
another such painting rested on an easel in the center of
the room, and around this easel a space had been cleared,
but the material that was banked against the walls and
rose all the way to the ceiling threatened to engulf it at
any moment. There were gilt picture frames, some as large
as a door; there were crocks and pails half filled with coagu-
lated liquids, cartons, milk bottles, splintered crates covered with layers of dust and tobacco crumbs, rolls of linen
canvas with rectangles ripped out, jugs of varnish and
turpentine lined up on an army cot with a broken leg,
brushes, rags, tubes, apple cores, wrappers of chocolate
bars, Brazil nuts, toothpicks, and pictures everywhere—

glued on the walls or on boxes or, it seemed, on whatever was closest: pictures of madonnas, airplanes, zebras, rapiers, gargoyles, schooners, adobe pueblos, and a host of others. There seemed to be no plan or preference; a solarized print of a turkey feather had been stuck to the trunk so that it half obliterated a sepia print of the Bosporus. The glue pot itself could be traced by its smell to a cobwebbed corner where, because it had cracked and was leaking, it sat on a piece of wrapping paper. On this paper was an inscription, printed at one time in red Conté but now almost invisible. Beneath the glue and ashes the letters read:

> I am here,
> I have traversed the Tomb,
> I behold thee,
> Thou who art strong!

Here and there on the floor lay bits of what looked like chalk but which were the remains of a little plaster cast of Michelangelo's *Bound Slave*. The fragments suggested that the statuette had not fallen but had been thrown to the floor. Also scattered about were phonograph records; most of them looked as if someone had bitten them. Several rested on the collar of a shaggy overcoat which in turn was draped over a stepladder. The phonograph itself lay on its side, the crank jutting up like the skeleton of a bird's wing and the splintered megaphone protruding from beneath one corner of a mattress like some great ear. In the middle of the night when the university campus was totally deserted there would occasionally come from the rear of North Fayer Hall the muffled sound of plain-song or

Gregorian chant, to which was sometimes added for a few bars a resonant bass voice in absolute harmony, that of the instructor whose name was printed in gold on the studio door, a door that was always locked: ANDREV ANDRAUKOV, DRAWING & PAINTING.

Nothing interested Andraukov except paint. Each thing he saw or heard or touched, whether it writhed like a sensuous woman or lay cold as an empty jug, did not live for him until he, by his own hand, had given it life. Wherever he happened to be, in a class or outside, he paced back and forth like a tiger, and when with hands laced into a knot at the tail of his sack-like tweed coat and his huge, bony head bowed as if in prayer he stalked the corridors of North Fayer Hall, or the streets of Davenport below the university, he created a silence. Always he walked with his head bowed, and so far had his slanting eyes retreated into their sockets that few people had met his gaze. His teeth were as yellow and brown as his leathery skin and it seemed as if flesh were too much of a luxury for his bones to endure.

It was his habit to start each drawing class in the still life room, a damp, chill studio with shelf upon shelf of plaster and bronze casts. He always took his students there the first morning; they stood about uncertainly, their young faces rosy from the September air, clean pencils and papers and new drawing boards clutched in their arms.

"Here," he would say, unrolling a long, cold finger. "Rome. Egypt. Greece. Renaissance. You will copy."

The students looked at him, a haggard old man whose head by daylight could be no more than a skull in a leather bag, and one by one they settled themselves before a statue. Around and around behind them went Andrev Andraukov, taking from awkward fingers the pencils or sticks of charcoal, drawing with incredible delicacy tiny explanatory sketches in a corner of the paper. When he leaned down to inspect the drawings of the girls they stiffened and held their breath fearing he might somehow contaminate them. To them he might have been the Genghis Khan. Slowly and with a kind of infinite patience he wandered from one to another, shaking his head, trying to explain, never taking from his mouth the stub of a brown cigarette which protruded from his drooping and streaked mustache like an unfortunate tooth. The moment he heard the chimes which ended each class he halted his explanation even though in the middle of a sentence, and without a single word or another look he went out. The sound of his footsteps echoing in the corridor ended with what seemed like the closing of a hundred distant doors.

When he saw that his students were losing interest in the plasters and so could gain nothing more, he took them into the life atelier. On the walls of this room were tacked reproductions of masterful paintings. Helter-skelter stood drawing boards and student paintings, and on a platform rested an electric heater and a stool. Here, in this studio, he commenced his instruction of the living human body: on the blackboard he drew diagrams and explained for several days, as best he could through the net of language, how it was that men and women functioned. Then he got his students a model. Each morning one would arrive carrying a little satchel in which there was a robe or a cloak to wear during the rest periods and sometimes an apple or cigarettes or even a book.

Generally the models did as others had done for three thousand years before them, so there faced the class each morning a noble though somewhat shopworn pose. With earnest faces the students copied, bending down close to their paper the better to draw each eyelash and mole, their fingers clutching the charcoal as if they were engraving poetry on the head of a pin, and one after another they discovered that if charcoal was rubbed it would shine. In two days every drawing gleamed like the top of a candy box. All the while their instructor, a cigarette fixed in his smelly mustache, paced the back of the room or walked up and down the corridor.

Although the students did not know it, he was waiting. Year after year as students flowed by him this old man watched and waited; he waited for the one who might be able to understand what it meant to be an artist, one student, born with the instinct of compassion, who could learn, who would renounce temporal life for the sake of billions yet unborn, just one who cared less for himself than for others. But there were good foods to eat, dear friends to chat with, and pretty girls to be seduced, so many fascinating things to be done and discussed, thus Andrev Andraukov could only watch and wait.

It was as if a little play never ended, wherein, to his eternal question, *Is it not important?,* the young people answered, *Yes! Yes! There must be one who cares!* And he asked, *Will it be you, then?* But they replied, *Ah, no! Not me! Someone else. You see, I have so awfully many things to do. . . .*

One November morning the members of Andraukov's class found lettered on the blackboard in his square hand, TODAY: ANATOMY. As a result they did not open their lockers but sat in a semicircle facing the model stand and waited. Andraukov hurried in several minutes late; beside him walked a strange model who went behind the Japanese screen in the corner and began to undress.

Indicating a six-foot plaster man, stripped of skin and flesh, Andraukov asked two of the students to lift it onto the model stand. Next he pointed to the wooden cabinet where a skeleton dangled by a bolt through its skull, and said, "Mr. Bones." Two more students carried the rattling skeleton onto the stand. There was a half-smoked cigarette clamped in the jaws. Andraukov patiently removed it, as he had removed hundreds of others.

"Now," he said, "Miss Novak, please."

His model walked out from behind the screen and stepped onto the platform where she stood between the skeleton and the cut-away. She was a huge peasant girl with tubular limbs and coarse red hair that hung down her back like a rug. Between her great breasts was the tattoo of a ship. Her Slavic eyes were expressionless.

Andraukov took up a position behind the semicircle of students. From one of his coat pockets—which was more of a pouch—he brought up a crooked brown cigarette. After he had held two matches under it the cigarette began to sputter, flame, and finally emit blasts of terra-cotta smoke. Now Andraukov was ready to begin the lecture; he walked a few steps in each direction and then blew from his nostrils such a cloud that he nearly hid himself.

"Well," he began, "here is girl. Young woman. Who does not agree?" He walked out of the smoke, looked around, and then walked back into it. "Good. We progress. On street I look at woman first the head, then down, so we will do here. Who can tell what is the shape of human head? Mr. Sprinkle will tell us."

Sprinkle stood up and fingered his lower lip while he

thought. Finally he answered that the human head was shaped like a ball.

"So? Miss Vitale will tell us."

Alice Vitale said it looked like an egg.

"Miss Novak, please to turn around. We will see back of head."

The model gathered her hair and lifted it until the class could see her neck and the base of the skull.

"Mr. Bondon, now, please."

Michael Bondon had begun to grow sideburns, and because his father was very rich he was not afraid to cross his legs and shrug.

Andraukov watched him for several seconds and then without expression continued, "Ball. Egg. Who is correct?" He explained that from the front the human head does resemble an egg and from the rear a ball or a melon, but, he cautioned, the artist must not look at what he sees so much as what he cannot see, and holding up one hand he demonstrated that the students, seeing his palm with their eyes, must also see his knuckles with their minds. He said that the artist must see around corners and through walls, even as he must see behind smiles, behind looks of pain.

"For to what use you shall employ knowledge?" he asked, walking to the window and gazing out at the slopes covered with wet snow. "For what you shall be artist? To draw such as all the world can see? Pussycat? Nice bouquet of lily? Little boy in sailor suit? Then bring to this class a camera. No! Not to this class. Go elsewhere." He looked out the window again at the soggy clouds which were settling on the university buildings, and then with his cigarette pinched between thumb and forefinger as if it were alive and about to jump, he walked slowly across the room where he stopped with his back to the students. "You people, you wish to be artist. Why? That a stranger on the street will call you by name? You would be famous? You would have money? Or is it you have looked at your schedule and said, 'Ah, this is hard! I need now something easy. Yes, I will take drawing.' "

He turned around, looked at the faces of the men, his gaze resting on each for a number of seconds. "You have thought, 'I will take drawing because in studio will be pretty girl without dress!' So? This is reason? Or perhaps in this room—in this room perhaps now there sits young man who in this world discovers injustice. He would be conscience of the world. Mr. Dillon will now stand up. Mr. Dillon, you would draw picture which is to say, 'Behold! Injustice!'? You would do that?"

"No, sir," Dillon murmured.

"You will not be conscience of the world?"

"No, sir."

"If not you," Andraukov asked, gazing at the boy, "then who?" He carefully licked the under side of his mustache and pushed the cigarette deeper into his mouth. His knuckles were yellow and hard as stone. From the town of Davenport the sound of automobile horns came faintly up to the university hills; but for these noises and the creak of the instructor's shoes the life studio was quiet.

Andraukov walked to the stand where he flattened his thumb against the neck of the cut-away. "Sterno-mastoid. Favorite muscle. Favorite muscle of art student." He asked his model to look at the skeleton and as she turned her head the sterno-mastoid stretched like a rope between ear and collarbone.

"*Beatrice d'Este,* how many know this painting, painting by Leonardo da Vinci? Three? Three hands? Disgrace! Now I tell you: In *Beatrice* is no sterno-mastoid. And why? Leonardo da Vinci is painting young woman, is not painting tackle of football team." He looked down on the faces turned attentively toward him and did not think they understood, but he did not know how to phrase it any more clearly. He decided to tell a joke. With a piece of green chalk he sketched on the blackboard a grotesque profile. He peered at it and shouted, "Young man after my daughter. Look like this! No, no—" He had confused the grammar. "Would have daughter, such young man like this." The class did not know what he was doing.

Andraukov felt he should explain his joke. He pulled on his mustache for a while and tried again but there was still only a confused tittering. He decided to continue with the lecture. Having become a trifle warm he unbuttoned his vest and hooked both thumbs in the pockets.

"Well, below head is neck. Below neck is breast. You are afraid of this word. Why? This is God's word. Why everybody—all the young girls say 'bust'? Bust is for fire-cracker. Not for woman. No! Everybody—class entire to-gether—now say correct word."

He listened to the class uneasily repeat the word and he nodded with satisfaction. "So! Not to be 'bust' again. I do not like that word. For drawing; art student draw like balloon. This is wrong. Not balloon, but is bag to rest on rib cage. Is part of body like ear is part of head, like peanut butter of sandwich, not to be alone. Who does not understand? Who has question?" No hands were raised.

Andraukov asked his model to face him with her heels

together, legs straight, and hands at her sides. He stared. He was pleased with the way she stood.

"Class. Class, consider Miss Novak, fine model, head high. Is good to be proud of body. Yes. This is true!" He struck himself with a stony fist. "No scent on earth is so putrid as shame. Good students, do not fear to be proud." He paused to meditate. "Well, on rib who can tell status of breast? Nobody? There is nobody to speak? There is fear?" He looked around. "Ah! Brave student. Mr. Zahn will speak. Mr. Zahn stands to tell instructor of breast. Good. Speak." With head bowed he prepared to listen, but almost immediately held up one hand. "No, no! I would know direction. I would know angle. Yes, angle. On breast does nipple look ahead like nose on face?"

Logan Zahn was a thin, heavily bearded young man who sat in corners whenever possible. He was older than the other students and wore glasses so thick that his eyes seemed to bulge. There were rumors that he was writing a book about something.

"No," he answered in a surprisingly high voice.

"The nipple, it will look down, perhaps?"

"No."

"Then where?"

"Up."

"And?"

"Out."

"Good!"

Zahn and the model looked at each other, both expressionless.

"You will tell instructor amount of angle. The left breast now, to where it is looking?"

"At the print of Cézanne's apples on the wall."

"And the right?"

Logan Zahn was not afraid. He pointed out the window. "At the Episcopal church."

Andraukov looked at the model and then toward the church. "That is correct." He tugged from his vest a heavy watch and studied it, pursing his lips. Why, he asked, tucking away the watch, why was it that men wished to touch women? To allow time for his question to penetrate he folded his arms across his chest and began wandering about the studio. He picked a bit of chalk off the floor, he opened a window an inch, he stroked a dusty bronze on a shelf, he went back to close the window, and when at last he felt that every student should have been able to consider his question and speak of it properly he invited answers. Nobody volunteered.

"I will tell you," he said. "No, I will not tell you. Mr. Van Antwerp will stand."

Van Antwerp, who was the university's wrestling champion, scratched his scalp and grinned. Andraukov's face did not move.

Van Antwerp grinned some more. "They're fat," he said.

"Man is not fat? Yes, but different. Well, on woman where it is most thick?"

Van Antwerp began to stand on his other foot. He blushed and sniggered. The class was silent. For a few moments Andraukov stood with eyes closed and head cocked to one side as if listening to something beyond the range of other ears, but abruptly he strode across the room to Van Antwerp's green tin locker and wrenched it open.

"These material, it belong to you? Take it now. You will not return! Who else now—who else—" But not being able to phrase what he wished to say he stood facing a shelf while Van Antwerp collected his things and left, slamming the door. Andraukov looked over his shoulder at the students. He turned all the way around and the color began to come back into his face.

"We speak of shape. Shape, yes. Is caused by many things. There is fat, placed by God, to protect child of womb. There is pelvic structure—so broad!" His bony hands gripped an imaginary pelvis. "There is short leg, spinal curve so deep. There is, too, the stance of woman. All these things, these things are not of man. You will not draw man and on him put balloons, lipstick, hair, and so to say, 'Here is woman!' No!"

He continued that woman was like the turtle, born to lie in the sun and sometimes to be turned over. Woman, he told them, was passive. She was not to smoke tobacco, to swear, to talk to man, to dance with man, to love like a drunken sailor; she was to brush her hair and wait. As he thought about the matter Andrev Andraukov stalked back and forth cutting the layers of smoke left by his cigarette.

"Trouser! Crop hair! Drink beer! For ten thousand years woman is correct: gentle, quiet, fat. Now?" He paused to stare at the floor, then lifting his head, said, "Well, today is good model. Consider limbs: not little to break in pieces but big and round like statue of Egyptian goddess, like statue in concrete like *Girl Holding Fruit* of Clodion. This piece, how many know? This Clodion?" He looked over the class and seeing only two hands pinched the bridge of his nose in a sudden, curious gesture and closed his eyes. He instructed them all to go to the library that afternoon and find a picture of the statue. Around the studio he wandered like a starved and shabby friar, the cuffs of his fray-

ing trousers dusting the paint-stained boards and the poor
coat dangling from the knobs of his shoulders. The laces
of his shoes had been broken and knotted many times, the
heels worn round. He stopped in a corner beside a cast of
St. George by Donatello and passed his fingertips across the
face as if he were making love to it. He licked the drooping corner hairs of his mustache. He swung his Mongol
head toward the class.

"You do not know Clodion! You do not know Signorelli,
Perugino, Hokusai, Holbein! You do not even know Da
Vinci, not even Cranach or Dürer! How, then, how I can
teach you? Osmosis? You will look inside my head? Each
day you sit before the model to draw. I watch. There is
ugly model, I see on your face nothing. Not pity, not re-
volt, not wonder. Nothing. There is beautiful model, like
today. I see nothing. Not greed, not sadness, not even fever.
Students, have you love? Have you hate? Or these things
are words to you? As the artist feels so does he draw. I
look at you, I do not need to look at the drawing."

There was no sound but the footsteps of the old instructor. Dust motes whirled about him as he walked through
a bar of winter sunlight.

"Good students, why you have come to me? You do not
know what is crucifixion, the requiem, transfiguration.
You do not even know the simple ecstasy. These things I
cannot teach. No. I teach the hand. No man can teach the
heart." Holding up his own hand for them all to see he
went on, "This is not the home of the artist. Raphael does
not live here." Tapping himself on the chest he said, "The
home of Raphael is here."

The little sunlight faded so that all the sky was mush-
room gray, somehow auguring death and the winter. A

wind rose, rattling the windows. The studio's one radiator began to knock and send up jets of steam. Andraukov snapped on the lights. He walked toward the motionless Slavic woman, his eyes going up and down her body as he approached.

"Who can find for instructor, sartorius?"

A girl went to the plaster cast and spiraled one finger down its thigh.

"Now on the model."

She touched the crest of the hip and inside the knee.

"What Miss Grodsky does not say is, ilium to tibia. But is all right because she tries. She will learn."

He asked if anybody knew why the muscle was named sartorius, but nobody knew; he told them it came from the word *sartor,* which meant tailor, and that this muscle must be used in order to sit cross-legged as years ago the tailors used to sit. He asked for the patella and his student laid one finger on the model's kneecap but did not know what the word meant. It meant a little pan, he said, as he drew its outline on the model's skin with a stick of charcoal. He asked next for the scapula; she hesitated and then touched the collarbone. He shook his head, saying, "Not clavicle, not the key." She guessed at the ankle and he shook his head again, placing her finger behind the model's shoulder. There with charcoal he outlined the scapula, saying as he finished it, "So! And Miss Grodsky can sit down. Mr. Zahn will find for instructor, pectoralis major."

Logan Zahn got up again and pointed.

Andraukov said, "Miss Novak does not bite." He watched as Zahn placed a fingertip outside and then inside her breast. "Correct. Easy question." With charcoal he drew the pectoralis on her skin. "Now for instructor, gluteus medius." He watched Zahn touch the side of her hip.

"Gastrocnemius."

He patted the calf of her leg.

"Masseter."

He touched her jaw.

Andraukov looked at him intently. "You are medical student?"

"No."

"Find for me—find pectoralis minor."

With his hands Zahn indicated that it lay deeper in the body.

"So. Where you have learn what you know?"

"Library," Zahn answered in his squeaky voice.

"I have told you to study anatomy in library?"

"No."

"But you have gone?"

"Yes."

Andraukov's nostrils dilated and he blew a cloud of smoke dark enough to have come from a ship; he stood in the middle of it, nearly hidden. When he emerged he began to speak of the differences between men and women; placing both hands on the model's forehead he stretched the skin above her drugged eyes until the class saw how smooth the skull appeared, and for comparison he pointed to the ridge of bone like that of an ape's on the bleached skeleton. He pointed to the angle of the model's jawbone and next to the more acute angle on the skeleton. Below the pit of her neck he drew an outline of the sternum and compared it to the skeleton's longer, straighter bone. He said that the woman's neck seemed longer because the clavicle was shorter, thus narrowing the shoulders, that the elbow looked higher because the female humerus was

short, that the reason one could not judge the height of
seated women was because they possessed great variations
in the length of the leg, that female buttocks were of
greater diameter than male because of protective fat and
because the sacrum assumes a greater angle. He turned the
skeleton about on its gallows and placed his model in the
same position. He drew the sacrum on her skin, and the
vertebrae rising above it. She arched her back so that he
could lay his hand on the sloping shelf. Why, he asked,
why was it thus? And he answered himself, saying that the
spine of man was straighter. Then for what reason did the
spine of woman curve? For what reason did the pelvis tilt?
Who would explain to him?

But again he answered himself. "Cushion!" A cushion
for the foetus. From a cupboard he brought a length of
straight wire and stabbed it at the floor; the wire twanged
and vibrated from the shock, but after he had bent it into
an *S* the wire bounced. He flung it into a corner and
walked back and forth rubbing his hands as he lectured.
The belly protrudes because there resides the viscera of
the human body. Fashion magazines do not know about
viscera, they print pictures of young girls who cannot eat
because they have no stomach, who cannot walk because
they have no maximus, who seem to stand on broken
ankles. Although paper was flat the students must draw
as if it were round; they must draw not in two dimensions
but in three. A good artist could draw in three dimensions,
a master could draw in four.

He stopped to consider the attentive looks on their faces
and asked who understood, but did not wait for an answer.
He spoke of how Rembrandt painted a young woman looking out an open window and said to them that she did not

live three hundred years ago, no, she was more than one young woman, she was all, from the first who had lived on earth to the one yet unborn who would be the final. He told them that some afternoon they would glance up by chance and see her; then they would know the meaning of Time—what it could destroy, what it could not. But for today, he said, his voice subsiding, three dimensions would be enough. From his baggy vest he extracted a silver thimble. He held it between two fingers.

"For belly, three dimensions. It is not, like paper, flat. So navel is not black dot. It is deep. It is the eye of God. You are going to see." Bending down he pushed the thimble steadily into the model's navel.

Every little noise in the studio ceased. There was no movement. It seemed an evil spell had been thrown by the thimble which retreated and advanced toward the students in brief, glittering arcs.

Andraukov licked his yellow mustache. "Good students, you will forget again?"

The class was still paralyzed. Waves of shock swept back and forth across the room; with the elongated senses of the mystic Andraukov caught them.

"Good students," he said simply. "Listen. Now I speak. You have come to me not to play. You have come to learn. I will teach. You will learn. Good students, each time in history that people have shame, each time in history that people hide from what they are, then in that age there is no meaning to life. There is imitation. Nothing more. There is nothing from which the little generation can learn. There is no weapon for the son to take from the hands of his father to conquer the forces of darkness and so to bring greatness to the people of earth."

Andrev Andraukov put the thimble back in his vest pocket. The thin soles of his pointed, paint-spattered shoes flapped on the boards as he walked to the cast of *St. George* and stood for a time gazing absently beyond it.

Suddenly he asked, "Will you like to hear a story?" and immediately began telling it.

Eleven years ago he had taught another drawing class much like their own where the students drew stiff, smudgy pictures of Greek warriors and made spaghetti of Michelangelo's muscles. But they, too, had worked hard, it had been a good class, and so one day he brought them into the life studio and gave them a woman. He left them alone that first morning and when he returned at noon they lined their drawing boards up against the wall and waited for his criticism.

In regard to the first drawing he observed that the head looked as big as a watermelon and he explained that the human head was nearly the same length as the foot; immediately the class members discovered they had drawn the feet too small. The hand, he told them, demonstrating, would more than cover the face; the class laughed at the tiny hands on all the drawings. How could they have made such mistakes! Well, they would learn.

At the second piece of work he stood facing them with hands at his sides and in a few moments the class discovered what he was doing: they had not drawn the arms long enough. He explained the various uses of the human arm, suggesting that if they would learn to speak truly of function then their drawings would be correct. He looked at their faces and saw the struggle to comprehend. It was a good class.

The next drawing was a tiny thing but when he bent

down to peer at it he discovered the streaks which were meant to be veins in the back of the model's hand. He held out his own hand with its great veins of red and green twine.

"These are important?" he asked them, and as he lifted his hands high in the air the class watched the veins recede.

So one by one he criticized those first works. When he came to the final drawing he found the figure had been covered by a bathing suit. He thought it was a joke. He turned to the class with a puzzled smile, but seeing their faces he knew it was not a joke.

"Who has drawn this?" he asked. No hand was raised. He returned to the first drawing and asked its owner to leave the studio; he stopped at the second drawing and asked its owner to leave. One by one the students walked out and finally he was left with two drawings but only one student.

"Miss Hugasian," he said, "you draw this morning two pictures?"

She pointed to the first.

"Well, then, this final drawing?"

Her eyes were brilliant with fright but he was patient and at last she said it had been done by Patricia Bettencourt.

"Miss Bettencourt? She is here today?" Then he left the studio and walked up and down the corridor opening each door until finally in the still-life room, seated between the casts of *Night* and *Day* with a handkerchief held over her face he saw Patricia Bettencourt. Looking down on her he wondered.

She did not move.

"You are ill?" he asked, bringing a bench close to her

and sitting down. "For me today you make very nice drawing, but the bathing suit—"

Andraukov paused in telling the story of Patricia Bettencourt, but he did not stop pacing so the eyes of the students swung steadily back and forth. Once again the only sounds in the atelier were the creak of his shoes and the knocking radiator. From time to time the electric heater on the model's platform hummed faintly. Rain trickled down the window panes and, finding cracks in the ancient putty, seeped and dripped to the floor where puddles were spreading. Before continuing with the story he walked to the door and opened it.

"Miss Bettencourt speaks. 'I did not know model was to be—' This sentence she cannot finish because she weeps. I finish for her. I ask, 'Nude?' She does not answer. Shadow like shroud drops on cast of Michelangelo."

Andraukov tasted his mustache and nodded to himself. He walked to the window where he stood with his back to the class; they could see only the thin hair on his skull and his yellow fingers tied into a knot at the tail of his coat.

"Good pupils, the artist is not 'nice.' No, that cannot be. He shall hear at times the voice of God, at times the shriek of each dwarf in the heart and in the soul, and shall obey those voices. But the voice of his fellow man? No. That cannot be. I think he who would create prepares his cross. Yes! It is so. But at his feet no Magdalen. Who, then, shall accuse: 'You are evil!'? 'You are sublime!'? There is no one to speak these words. Miss Bettencourt is in this room? Go now. I do not wish to see your face."

The door to the corridor stood open. Andraukov remained at the window with his back to the students.

"Then I will teach you. I teach of the human body and

of the human soul. Now you are young, as once even I was. Even as yours were my nostrils large. Now you shall learn what is the scent of life, and with fingers to touch, with ears to listen. Each fruit you shall taste, of honey and grape, and one day persimmon. I, too, have kissed the hot mouth of life, have shattered the night with cries, have won through such magic millions of years. You will listen now! God is just. He gives you birth. He gives you death. He bids you to look, to learn, and so to live."

The chimes of the university chapel had begun to toll. Wrapping his fingers once again into a knot at the tail of his coat Andrev Andraukov walked out the door. The anatomy lesson was over.

The Beau Monde of Mrs. Bridge

Parking

The black Lincoln that Mr. Bridge gave her on her forty-seventh birthday was a size too long and she drove it as cautiously as she might have driven a locomotive. People were always blowing their horns at her or turning their heads to stare when they went by. The Lincoln had been set to idle too slowly, and in consequence the engine sometimes died when she pulled up at an intersection, but as her husband never used the Lincoln and she herself assumed it was just one of those things about automobiles, the idling speed was never adjusted. Often she would delay a line of cars while she pressed the starter button either too long or not long enough. Knowing she was not expert she was always quite apologetic when something unfortunate happened, and did her best to keep out of everyone's way. She changed into second gear at the beginning of any hill and let herself down the far side much more slowly than necessary.

Usually she parked in a downtown garage where Mr. Bridge rented a stall for her. She had only to honk at the enormous doors, which would then trundle open, and coast on inside where an attendant would greet her by name, help her out, and then park the formidable machine. But in the country-club district she parked on the street, and if there were diagonal stripes she did very well, but if parking was parallel she had trouble judging her distance from the curb and would have to get out and walk around to look, then get back in and try again. The Lincoln's seat was so soft and Mrs. Bridge so short that she had to sit very erect in order to see what was happening ahead of her. She drove with arms thrust forward and gloved hands tightly on the large wheel, her feet just able to depress the pedals all the way. She never had serious accidents but was often seen here and there being talked to by patrolmen. These patrolmen never did anything, partly because they saw immediately that it would not do to arrest her and partly because they could tell she was trying to do everything the way it should be done.

When parking on the street it embarrassed her to have people watch, yet there always seemed to be someone at the bus stop or lounging in a doorway with nothing to do but stare while she struggled with the wheel and started jerkily backward. Sometimes, however, there would be a nice man who, seeing her difficulty, would come around and tip his hat and ask if he might help.

"Would you, please?" she would ask in relief, and after he opened the door she would get out and stand on the curb while he put the car in place. It was a problem to know whether he expected a tip or not. She knew that people who stood around on the streets were in need of money, still she did not want to offend anyone. Sometimes she would hesitantly ask, sometimes not, and whether the man would accept a twenty-five-cent piece or no she would smile brightly up at him, saying, "Thank you so much," and having locked the Lincoln's doors she would be off to the shops.

Minister's Book

If Mrs. Bridge bought a book it was almost always one of three things: a best seller she had heard of or seen advertised in all the stores, a self-improvement book, or a book by a Kansas City author no matter what it was about. These latter were infrequent, but now and again someone would explode on the midst of Kansas City with a Civil War history or something about old Westport Landing. Then, too, there were slender volumes of verse and essays usually printed by local publishing houses, and it was one of these that lay about the living room longer than any other book with the exception of an extremely old two-volume set of *The Brothers Karamazov* in gold-painted leather which nobody in the house had ever read and which had been purchased from an antique dealer by Mr. Bridge's brother. This set rested gravely on the mantel-piece between a pair of bronze Indian-chief heads—the only gift from cousin Lulubelle Watts that Mrs. Bridge had ever been able to use—and was dusted once a week by Hazel with a peacock-feather duster.

The volume that ran second to *The Brothers Karamazov* was a collection of thoughts by the local minister, Dr. Foster, a short and congenial and even jovial man with a big, handsome head capped with soft golden white hair which he allowed to grow long and which he brushed toward the top of his head to give himself another inch or so. He had written these essays over a period of several years with the idea of putting them into book form, and from time to time would allude to them, laughingly, as his memoirs. Then people would exclaim that he surely mustn't keep them to himself until he died, at which Dr. Foster, touching the speaker's arm, would laugh heartily and say, "We'll think it over, we'll think it over," and clear his throat.

At last, when he had been preaching in Kansas City for seventeen years and his name was recognized, and he was often mentioned in *The Tattler* and sometimes in the city paper, a small publishing firm took these essays which he had quietly submitted to them several times before. The book came out in a black cover with a dignified gray and purple dust jacket that showed him smiling pensively out of his study window at dusk, hands clasped behind his back and one foot slightly forward.

The first essay began, "I am now seated at my desk, the desk that has been a source of comfort and inspiration to me these many years. I see that night is falling, the shadows creeping gently across my small but (to my eyes) lovely garden, and at such times as this I often reflect on the state of Mankind."

Mrs. Bridge read Dr. Foster's book, which he had autographed for her, and was amazed to find that he was such a reflective man, and so sensitive to the sunrise which she discovered he often got up to watch. She underlined several passages in the book that seemed to have particular meaning for her, and when it was done she was able to discuss it with her friends, who were all reading it, and she recommended it strongly to Grace Barron, who at last consented to read a few pages.

With ugly, negative books about war and Communists and perversion and everything else constantly flooding the counters this book came to her like an olive branch. It assured her that life was worth living after all, that she had not and was not doing anything wrong, and that people needed her. So, in the shadow of Dostoevski, the pleasant meditations of Dr. Foster lay in various positions about the living room.

Maid from Madras

The Bridges gave an evening party not because they wanted to have cocktails with a mob of people, but because it was about time for them to be giving a party. Altogether more than eighty people stood and wandered about the home which stood on a hillside and was in the style of a Loire Valley chateau. Grace and Virgil Barron were there, Madge and Russ Arlen, the Heywood Duncans, Welhelm and Susan Van Metre looking out of place, Lois and Stuart Montgomery, the Beckerle sisters in ancient beaded gowns and looking as though they had not an instant forgotten the day when Mrs. Bridge had entertained them in anklets, Noel Johnson huge and by himself because she was in bed suffering from exhaustion, Mabel Ong trying to start serious discussions, Dr. and Mrs. Batchelor whose Austrian refugee guests were now domestics in Los Angeles, and even Dr. Foster, smiling tolerantly, who appeared for a whisky sour and a cigarette while gently chiding several of the men about Sunday golf. There was also an auto salesman named Beachy Marsh who had arrived early in a double-breasted pin-stripe business suit instead of a tuxedo, and being embarrassed about his mistake did everything he could think of to be amusing. He was not a close friend but it had been necessary to invite him along with several others.

Mrs. Bridge rustled about the brilliantly lighted home checking steadily to see that everything was as it should be. She glanced into the bathrooms every few minutes and found that the guest towels, which resembled pastel handkerchiefs, were still immaculately overlapping one another on the rack—at evening's end only three had been disturbed—and she entered the kitchen once to recommend that the extra servant girl, hired to assist Hazel, pin shut the gap in the breast of her starched uniform.

Through the silver candelabra and miniature turkey sandwiches Mrs. Bridge went graciously smiling and chatting a moment with everyone, quietly opening windows to let out the smoke, removing wet glasses from mahogany table tops, slipping away now and then to empty the onyx ashtrays she had bought and distributed throughout the house.

Beachy Marsh got drunk. He slapped people on the shoulder, told jokes, laughed loudly, and also went around emptying the ashtrays of their cherry-colored stubs, all the while attempting to control the tips of his shirt collar which had become damp from perspiration and were rolling up into the air like horns. Following Mrs. Bridge halfway up the carpeted stairs he said hopefully, "There was a young maid from Madras, who had a magnificent ass; not rounded and pink, as you probably think—it was gray, had long ears, and ate grass."

"Oh, my word!" replied Mrs. Bridge, looking over her

shoulder with a polite smile but continuing up the stairs, while the auto salesman plucked miserably at his collar.

Laundress in the Rear

Every Wednesday the laundress came, and as the bus line was several blocks distant from the Bridge home someone would almost always meet her bus in the morning. For years the laundress had been an affable old Negress named Beulah Mae who was full of nutshell wisdom and who wore a red bandanna and a dress that resembled a dyed hospital gown. Mrs. Bridge was very fond of Beulah Mae, speaking of her as "a nice old soul" and frequently giving her a little extra money or an evening dress that had begun to look dated, or perhaps some raffle tickets that she was always obliged to buy from Girl Scouts and various charities. But there came a day when Beulah Mae had had enough of laundering, extra gifts or no, and without saying a word to any of her clients she boarded a bus for California to live out her life on the seashore. For several weeks Mrs. Bridge was without a laundress and was obliged to take the work to an establishment, but at last she got someone else, an extremely large and doleful Swedish woman who said during the interview in the kitchen that her name was Ingrid and that for eighteen years she had been a masseuse and liked it much better.

When Mrs. Bridge arrived at the bus line the first morning Ingrid saluted her mournfully and got laboriously into the front seat. This was not the custom, but such a thing was difficult to explain because Mrs. Bridge did not like to hurt anyone's feelings by making them feel inferior, so she said nothing about it and hoped that by next week some other laundress in the neighborhood would have told Ingrid.

But the next week she again got in front, and again Mrs. Bridge pretended everything was all right. However on the third morning while they were riding up Ward Parkway toward the house Mrs. Bridge said, "I was so attached to Beulah Mae. She used to have the biggest old time riding in the back seat."

Ingrid turned a massive yellow head to look stonily at Mrs. Bridge. As they were easing into the driveway she spoke, "So you want I should sit in the back."

"Oh, gracious! I didn't mean that," Mrs. Bridge answered, smiling up at Ingrid. "You're perfectly welcome to sit right here if you like."

Ingrid said no more about the matter and next week with the same majestic melancholy rode in the rear.

Frayed Cuffs

Ordinarily Mrs. Bridge examined the laundry but when she had shopping to do, or a meeting, the job fell to Hazel who never paid much attention to such things as missing buttons or loose elastic. Thus it was that Mrs. Bridge discovered her son wearing a shirt with cuffs that were noticeably frayed.

"For Heaven's sake!" she exclaimed, taking hold of his sleeve. "Has a dog been chewing on it?"

He looked down at the threads as though he had never before seen them.

"Surely you don't intend to *wear* that shirt?"

"It looks perfectly okay to me," said Douglas.

"Just look at those cuffs! Anyone would think we're on our way to the poorhouse."

"So is it a disgrace to be poor?"

"*No!*" she cried. "But we're *not* poor!"

Equality

Mrs. Bridge approved of equality. On certain occasions when she saw in the newspapers or heard over the radio that labor unions had won another victory she would think, Good for them! And, as the segregational policies of the various states became more and more subject to criticism by civic groups as well as by the federal government, she would feel that it was about time, and she would try to understand how discrimination could persist. However strongly she felt about this she was careful about what she said because she was aware that everything she had was hers through the efforts of one person: her husband. Mr. Bridge was of the opinion that people were not equal. In his decisive manner of speaking, annoyed that she should even puzzle over such a thing, he said, "You take all the people on earth and divide up everything, and in six months everybody would have just about what they have now. What Abraham Lincoln meant was equal rights, not equal capacity."

This always seemed exactly what she was trying to point out to him, that many people did not have equal rights, but after a few minutes of discussion she would be overwhelmed by a sense of inadequacy and would begin to get confused, at which he would stare at her for a moment as though she were something in a glass box and then resume whatever he had been doing.

She invariably introduced herself to members of minority groups at gatherings where she found herself associating with them.

"I'm India Bridge," she would say in a friendly manner, and would wish it were possible to invite the people into her home. And when, among neighborhood friends she had known for a long time and who offered no unusual ideas, the increased means of certain classes were discussed, she would say, "Isn't it nice that they can have television and automobiles and everything."

In a northern town a Negro couple opened a grocery store in a white neighborhood; that night the windows were smashed and the store set afire. Newspapers published photographs of the ruined property, of two smirking policemen, and of the Negro couple who had lost their entire savings. Mrs. Bridge read this story while having breakfast by herself several hours after her husband had left for work. She studied the miserable faces of the young Negro and his wife. Across the newspaper the morning sun slanted warm and cheerful, in the kitchen Hazel sang hymns while peeling apples for a pie, all the earth as seen from her window seemed content, yet such things still came to pass. In her breakfast nook, a slice of buttered toast in hand, Mrs. Bridge felt a terrible desire. She would press these unfortunate people to her breast and tell them that she, too, knew what it meant to be hurt but that everything would turn out all right.

Gloves

She had always done a reasonable amount of charity
work along with her friends, particularly at a little store
on Ninth Street where second-hand clothing that had been
collected in drives was distributed. In this store were two
rooms; in the front one a row of card tables were placed together, behind which stood the charity workers who were
to assist people seeking something to wear, and in the
back room were several more card tables and collapsible
wooden chairs where Mrs. Bridge and her fellow workers
ate their lunch or relaxed when not on duty in front.

She often went down with Madge Arlen. One week
they would drive to their work in the Arlens' Chrysler,
the next week in Mrs. Bridge's Lincoln, and when this was
the case Mrs. Bridge always drew up before the garage
where her parking stall was rented. She honked, or beck-
oned if someone happened to be in sight, and shortly an
attendant whose name was George would come out buttoning up his jacket and he would ride in the rear seat to the
clothing store. There he would jump out and open the
door for Mrs. Bridge, and after that he would drive the
Lincoln back to the garage because she did not like it left
on the street in such a neighborhood.

"Can you come by for us around six, or six-fifteen-ish,
George?" she would ask.

He always answered that he would be glad to, touched
the visor of his cap, and drove away.

"He seems so nice," said Mrs. Arlen as the two of them
walked into their store.

"Oh, he is!" Mrs. Bridge agreed. "He's one of the nicest garage men I've ever had."

"How long have you been parking there?"

"Quite some time. We used to park at that awful place on Walnut."

"The one with the popcorn machine? Lord, isn't that the limit?"

"No, not that place. The one with the Italians. You know how my husband is about Italians. Well, that just seemed to be headquarters for them. They came in there to eat their sandwiches and listen to some opera broadcast from New York. It was just impossible. So finally Walter said, 'I'm going to change garages.' So we did."

They walked past the row of card tables piled high with soiled and sour unwashed clothing and continued into the back room where they found some early arrivals having coffee and éclairs. Mrs. Bridge and Mrs. Arlen hung up their coats and also had coffee, and then prepared for work. The reform school had sent down some boys to assist and they were put to work untying the latest sacks of used clothing and dumping them out.

By two o'clock everything was ready for the day's distribution. The doors were unlocked and the first of the poor entered and approached the counter behind which stood Mrs. Bridge and two others with encouraging smiles, all three of them wearing gloves.

Robbery at Heywood Duncans'

The Bridges were almost robbed while attending a cocktail party at the Heywood Duncans'. Shortly after ten o'clock, just as she was taking an anchovy cracker from the buffet table, four men appeared in the doorway with revolvers and wearing plastic noses attached to horn-rimmed glasses for disguise. One of them said, "All right, everybody. This is a stick-up!" Another of the men—Mrs. Bridge afterward described him to the police as not having worn a necktie—got up on the piano bench and from there stepped up on top of the piano itself where he pointed his gun at different people. At first everybody thought it was a joke, but it wasn't because the robbers made them all line up facing the wall with their hands above their heads. One of them ran upstairs and came down with his arms full of fur coats and purses while two others started around the room pulling billfolds out of the men's pockets and drawing rings from the ladies' fingers. Before they had gotten to either Mr. or Mrs. Bridge, who were lined up between Dr. Foster and the Arlens, something frightened them and the one standing on the piano called out in an ugly voice, "Who's got the keys to that blue Cadillac out front?"

At this Mrs. Ralph Porter screamed, "Don't you tell him, Ralph!"

But the bandits took Mr. Porter's keys anyway and after telling them all not to move for thirty minutes they ran out the porch door.

It was written up on the front page of the newspaper, with pictures on page eight, including a close-up of the scratched piano. Mrs. Bridge, reading the story in the breakfast room next morning after her husband had gone to work, was surprised to learn that Stuart Montgomery had been carrying just $2.14 and that Mrs. Noel Johnson's ring had been zircon.

Follow Me Home

How the scare actually started no one knew, although several women, one of whom was a fairly close friend of Madge Arlen, claimed they knew the name of someone who had been assaulted not far from Ward Parkway. Some thought it had happened near the Plaza, others thought farther south, but they were generally agreed that it had happened late at night. The story was that a certain lady of a well-known family had been driving home alone and when she had slowed down for an intersection a man had leaped up from behind some shrubbery and had wrenched open the door. Whether the attack had been consummated or not the story did not say; the important part was that there had been a man and he had leaped up and wrenched open the door. There was nothing in the paper about it, nor in *The Tattler,* which did not print anything unpleasant, and the date of the assault could not be determined for some reason, only that it had been on a dark night not too long ago.

When this story had gotten about none of the matrons wished to drive anywhere alone after sundown. As it so happened they were often obliged to go to a cocktail party or a dinner by themselves because their husbands were working late at the office, but they went full of anxiety, with the car doors locked. It also became customary for the husband-host to get his automobile out of the garage at the end of an evening and then to follow the unescorted matrons back to their homes. Thus there could be seen processions of cars driving cautiously and rather like funerals across the boulevards of the country-club residential district.

So Mrs. Bridge came home on those evenings when her husband did not get back from the office in time, or when he was too tired and preferred to lie in bed reading vacation advertisements. At her driveway the procession would halt, engines idling, while she drove into the garage and came back out along the driveway so as to be constantly visible, and entered by the front door. Having unlocked it she would step inside, switch on the hall lights, and call to her husband, "I'm home!" Then, after he had made a noise of some kind in reply, she would flicker the lights a few times to show the friends waiting outside that she was safe, after which they would all drive off into the night.

Never Speak to Strange Men

On a downtown street just outside a department store a man said something to her. She ignored him. But at that moment the crowd closed them in together.

"How do you do?" he said, smiling and touching his hat.

She saw that he was a man of about fifty with silvery hair and rather satanic ears.

His face became red and he laughed awkwardly. "I'm Gladys Schmidt's husband."

"Oh, for heaven's sake!" Mrs. Bridge exclaimed. "I didn't recognize you."

Conrad

While idly dusting the bookcase one morning she paused
to read the titles and saw an old red-gold volume of Conrad that had stood untouched for years. She could not
think how it happened to be there. Taking it down she
looked at the flyleaf and found *"Ex Libris* Thomas
Bridge."

She remembered then that they had inherited some
books and charts upon the death of her husband's brother,
an odd man who had married a night-club entertainer and
later died of a heart attack in Mexico.

Having nothing to do that morning she began to turn
the brittle, yellowed pages and slowly became fascinated.
After standing beside the bookcase for about ten minutes
she wandered, still reading, into the living room where
she sat down and did not look up from the book until
Hazel came in to announce lunch. In the midst of one of
the stories she came upon a passage that had once been
underlined, apparently by Tom Bridge, which remarked
that some people go skimming over the years of existence
to sink gently into a placid grave, ignorant of life to the
last, without ever having been made to see all it may contain. She brooded over this fragment even while reading
further, and finally turned back to it again, and was staring
at the carpet with a bemused expression when Hazel
entered.

Mrs. Bridge put the book on the mantel, for she intended to read more of this perceptive man, but during the
afternoon Hazel automatically put Conrad back on the
shelf and Mrs. Bridge did not think of him again.

Voting

She had never gone into politics the way some women did who were able to speak with masculine inflections about such affairs as farm surplus and foreign subsidies. She always listened attentively when these things came up at luncheons or circle meetings; she felt her lack of knowledge and wanted to know more, and did intend to buckle down to some serious studying. But so many things kept popping up that it was difficult to get started, and then too she did not know exactly how one began to learn. At times she would start to question her husband but he refused to say much to her, and so she would not press the matter because after all there was not much she herself could accomplish.

This was how she defended herself to Mabel Ong after having incautiously let slip the information that her husband told her what to vote for.

Mabel Ong was flat as an adolescent but much more sinewy. Her figure was like a bud that had never managed to open. She wore tweed coats and cropped hair and frequently stood with hands thrust deep into her side pockets as if she were a man. She spoke short positive sentences, sometimes throwing back her head to laugh with a sound that reminded people of a dry reed splintering. She had many bitter observations in regard to capitalism, relating stories she had heard from unquestionable sources about women dying in childbirth because they could not afford the high cost of proper hospitalization or even the cost of insurance plans.

"If I ever have a child—" she was fond of beginning, and would then tear into medical fees.

She demanded of Mrs. Bridge, "Don't you have a mind of your own? Great Scott, woman, you're an adult. Speak out! We've been emancipated." Ominously she began rocking back and forth from her heels to her toes, hands clasped behind her back while she frowned at the carpet of the Auxiliary clubhouse.

"You're right," Mrs. Bridge apologized, discreetly avoiding the smoke Mabel Ong blew into the space between them. "It's just so hard to know *what* to think. There's so much scandal and fraud, and I suppose the papers only print what they want us to know." She hesitated, then, "How do you make up *your* mind?"

Mabel Ong removed the cigarette holder from her small cool lips. She considered the ceiling and then the carpet, as though debating on how to answer such a naïve question, and finally suggested that Mrs. Bridge might begin to grasp the fundamentals by a deliberate reading of certain books, which she jotted down on the margin of a tally card. Mrs. Bridge had not heard of any of these books except one and this was because its author was being investigated, but she decided to read it anyway.

There was a waiting list for it at the public library but she got it at a rental library and settled down to go through it with the deliberation that Mabel Ong had advised. The author's name was Zokoloff, which certainly sounded threatening, and to be sure the first chapter was about bribery in the circuit courts. When Mrs. Bridge had gotten far enough along to feel capable of speaking about it she left it quite boldly on the hall table; however Mr.

Bridge did not even notice it until the third evening. He thinned his nostrils, read the first paragraph, grunted once, and dropped it back onto the hall table. This was disappointing. In fact, now that there was no danger involved, she had trouble finishing the book. She thought it would be better in a magazine digest, but at last she did get through and returned it to the rental library, saying to the owner, "I can't honestly say I agree with it all but he's certainly well informed."

Certain arguments of Zokoloff remained with her and she found that the longer she thought about them the more penetrating and logical they became; surely it *was* time, as he insisted, for a change in government. She decided to vote liberal at the next election, and as time for it approached she became filled with such enthusiasm and anxiety that she wanted very much to discuss government with her husband. She began to feel confident that she could persuade him to change his vote also. It was all so clear to her, there was really no mystery to politics. However when she challenged him to discussion he did not seem especially interested, in fact he did not answer. He was watching a television acrobat stand on his thumb in a bottle and only glanced across at her for an instant with an annoyed expression. She let it go until the following evening when television was over, and this time he looked at her curiously, quite intently, as if probing her mind, and then all at once he snorted.

She really intended to force a discussion on election eve. She was going to quote from the book of Zokoloff. But he came home so late, so tired, that she had not the heart to upset him. She concluded it would be best to let him vote as he always had, and she would do as she herself wished; still, upon getting to the polls, which were conveniently located in the country-club shopping district, she became doubtful and a little uneasy. And when the moment finally came she pulled the lever recording her wish for the world to remain as it was.

The Condor and the Guests

In Peru a female condor was staked inside a wooden cage. Every so often a male bird would get into this trap and would then be sold to a zoo or a museum. One of these captured condors, however, was sold to an American, J. D. Botkin of Parallel, Kansas.

It cost Mr. Botkin a great deal of money to get his bird into the United States, but he had traveled quite a bit and was proud of his ability to get anything accomplished that he set his mind to. At his home in Parallel he had a chain fastened about the bird's neck. The other end of the chain was padlocked to a magnolia tree which he had had transplanted to his back yard from the French Quarter of New Orleans on an earlier trip.

All the rest of that first day the condor sat in the magnolia tree and looked across the fields of wheat, but just before sundown it lifted its wings and spread them to the fullest extent as if testing the wind; then with a slow sweep of utter majesty it rose into the air. It took a second leisurely sweep with its wings, and a third. However, on the third stroke it came to the end of the chain. Then it made a sort of gasping noise and fell to the earth while the magnolia swayed from the shock. After its fall the gigantic bird did not move until long after dark when it got to its feet and climbed into the tree. Next morning as the sun rose it was on the same branch, looking south like a gargoyle taken from the ramparts of some cathedral.

Day after day it sat in the magnolia tree without moving, but every sundown it tried to take off. A pan of meat left nearby was visited only by a swarm of flies.

Almost a week following the bird's arrival Mr. Botkin was eating lunch at the Jupiter Club when he met his friend, Harry Apple, and said to him, "You seen my bird yet?"

Harry Apple was a shrunken, bald-headed man who never had much to say. He answered Mr. Botkin's question by slowly shaking his head. Mr. Botkin then exclaimed that Harry hadn't lived, and clapping him on the shoulder said he was giving a dinner party on Wednesday—a sort of anniversary of the condor's first week in Kansas—and asked if Harry could make it.

After the invitation had been extended Harry Apple sat silently for almost a minute and stared into space. He had married a tall, smoke-haired ex-show-girl of paralyzing beauty and he understood that she was the reason for the invitations he received.

At last he nodded, saying in his melancholy voice, "Sure. I'll bring Mildred, too."

Mr. Botkin clapped him on the shoulder and proposed a toast, "To the condor!"

Harry sipped his drink and murmured, "Sure."

Mr. Botkin also got the Newtons and the Huddlestuns for dinner. He was not too pleased about the Huddlestuns; Suzie Huddlestun's voice always set him on edge and

"Tiny" was a bore. He had asked the Bagleys, but Chuck Bagley was going to an insurance convention in Kansas City. He had also asked the Gerlachs, the Ridges, and the Zimmermans, but none of them could make it, so he settled for Suzie and Tiny. They were delighted with the invitation.

On the evening of the party "Fig" Newton and his wife had not arrived by seven o'clock, so Mr. Botkin said to the others—Mildred and Harry Apple, and Suzie and Tiny Huddlestun, "Well, by golly, this calls for a drink!"

With cocktails in their hands the guests wandered down to the magnolia tree and stood in a half-circle, shaking the ice in their glasses and looking critically upward. The men stood a bit closer to the tree than the ladies did in order to show that they were not afraid of the condor. The ladies did not think the somber bird would do anything at all and they would rather have sat on the porch and talked.

Tiny Huddlestun was an enormous top-heavy man who had been a wrestler when he was young. His larynx had been injured by a vicious Turk during a match in Joplin, so that now his voice was a sort of quavering falsetto. He bobbled the ice in his glass with an index finger as big as a sausage and said in his falsetto, "That a turkey you got there, Botkin?"

His wife laughed and squeezed his arm. Even in platform shoes she did not come up to his chin, and the difference in their sizes caused people to speculate. She never listened to what he said but every time she heard his voice she laughed and squeezed him.

Mildred Apple said a little sulkily, "J. D., I want it to do something exciting." The cocktail was making her feel dangerous.

Mr. Botkin snapped his fingers. "By golly!" He swallowed the rest of his drink, took Harry's empty glass, and went back to the house. In a few minutes he returned with fresh drinks and a green and yellow parrot riding on his shoulder. Solemnly he announced, "This here's Caldwell."

"Caldwell?" shrieked Suzie Huddlestun, and began to laugh so hard that she clutched Tiny's coat for support.

Mr. Botkin was laughing, too, although he did not want to because he disliked Suzie. His belt went under his belly like a girth under a horse and as he laughed the belt creaked. It was several minutes before he could pat the perspiration from his strawberry face and gasp, "By golly!" He turned to the Apples who had stood by politely smiling, and explained, "Old Nowlin Caldwell at the Pioneer Trust."

"Caldwell," the parrot muttered, walking around on Mr. Botkin's shoulder.

Tiny Huddlestun had been hugging his wife. He released her and cleared his throat. "You going to eat that bird at Thanksgiving, Botkin?"

Mr. Botkin ignored him and said, leaning his head over next to the parrot, "Looky there, Caldwell, that condor don't even move. He's scared to death of you. You get on up there and tear him to pieces."

The parrot jumped to the ground and ran to the magnolia tree. The tree had not done well in the Kansas climate and was a stunted little thing with ragged bark and weak limbs which were turning their tips toward the ground. The parrot hooked its way up the trunk with no trouble, but at the lowest fork paused to watch the condor.

Mr. Botkin waved a hand as big as a spade.

The parrot went on up, more slowly however, stopping every few seconds to consider. Finally it crept out on the same limb and in a burst of confidence clamped its bright little claws into the wood beside the condor's talons. Then it imitated the black giant's posture and blinked down at the guests, which caused all of them except Harry Apple to break into laughter. The chain clinked. This alarmed the parrot; it whipped its head around and found itself looking into one of the condor's flat eyes.

"Eat 'im up!" Tiny shouted.

But the parrot fell out of the tree and ran toward the house, flailing its brilliant wings in the grass and screaming.

While his guests were still chuckling Mr. Botkin pointed far to the south where thunderheads were building up and said, "That's what the Andes look like."

The guests were all studying the familiar clouds when Fig Newton's sedan squeaked into the driveway. Mr. Botkin waved to Fig and his wife and went into the kitchen to get more drinks. To the colored girl Mrs. Botkin had hired for the evening he said, "Ever see a bird like that?"

The colored girl looked out the window immediately and answered with enthusiasm, "No, sir, Mr. Botkin!" But this did not seem to satisfy him so she added, "No sir, I sure never have!"

"You bet your sweet bottom you haven't." He was chipping some ice. "Because that's a condor."

"What's he eat?" she asked, but since he did not answer she felt it had been a silly question and turned her head away in shame.

Mr. Botkin shook up the drinks, bumped open the

screen door with his stomach, and carried the tray into the yard. After he had greeted Fig and Laura Newton he said, "That little darky in the kitchen is scared to death of this bird. She wouldn't come near it for the world."

Fig answered, "Generally speaking, colored people are like that." He had a nervous habit of twitching his nose each time he finished speaking, which was the reason that hundreds of high-school students spoke of him as "Rabbit" Newton.

"Make him fly, J. D.," Laura said. "I want to admire his strength!" She was dressed in imitation gypsy clothes with a purple bandanna tied around her hips and a beauty mole painted on her temple. She did a little gypsy step across the yard, shaking her head so the gold earrings bounced against her cheeks. She lifted her glass high in the air. "Oh, make him fly!"

"Yes, do," added Mildred Apple. She had finished her drink quickly when she saw Laura's costume and now she stood on one leg so that her hips curved violently.

Mrs. Botkin, an egg-shaped little woman with wispy white hair that lay on her forehead like valentine lace, looked at her husband and started to say something. Then she puckered her lips and stopped.

Fig had been waiting for a pause. Now he drew attention to himself and said in measured tones, "Ordinarily the Negro avoids things he does not understand."

There was a polite silence until his nose twitched.

Then Mr. Botkin, whose cheeks had been growing redder with each drink, said, "You know what its name is?"

"What?" cried Suzie.

"Sambo," put in Fig, imitating a drawl. A laugh trem-

bled at his lips, but nobody else laughed so he tasted his
drink.

"Sherlock Holmes?" guessed Laura. Only Suzie tittered
at this and Laura glanced at her sourly.

Mr. Botkin finally said, "Well, I'm going to tell you—
it's Samson."

He waited until the guests' laughter had died away and
then he told them that the name of the female in Peru was
Delilah. He joined the laughter this time, his belt creaking and the perspiration standing out all over his face.
When the guests had quieted down to head-wagging chuck-
les he said, "Well, by golly, I'll stir this Samson up!" He
picked some sticks off the grass and began tossing them
into the magnolia. At last one hit the condor's chest, but
the huge bird seemed to be asleep.

"The damn thing won't eat, either!" he exclaimed in a
gust of irritation.

"Won't *eat?*" shrilled Suzie Huddlestun, standing in the
circle of Tiny's arms. "Gee, what's it live on if it don't eat?"

Mr. Botkin ignored her.

Fig cleared his throat. Pointing upward he said, "If you
will look at that branch you'll see it is bent almost like a
strung bow."

Mrs. Botkin suddenly turned to her husband and laid a
hand on his sleeve. "Dear—"

Everybody looked at her in mild surprise, as always happened when she decided to say anything. She pressed a
wisp of hair back into place and breathed, "Why don't you
let the bird go?"

There was an uncomfortable pause, which Laura Newton broke by dancing around the back yard again. The

candy-stripe skirt sailed around her bony goose legs. "How
many want the condor to fly?" she asked, and thrusting her
glass high in the air she cried, "Vote!"

Tiny Huddlestun had been squeezing his wife, but now
he held his glass as high as possible without spilling the
liquor and looked around with pleasure, knowing that nobody was tall enough to match the height of his ballot.
Suzie's glass, clutched in her childlike hand, came just
above his ear.

Mildred Apple sulkily lifted hers and so did Fig. Mr.
Botkin had been watching with a curious sort of interest.
His glass had gone up as soon as Laura proposed the vote.
He looked at his wife and she quickly lifted hers.

"Harry?" Laura cried.

Harry Apple continued drinking.

Mrs. Botkin murmured, "I think dinner's ready." She
fluttered her hands about in weak desperation but nobody
looked at her.

Laura asked in a different tone, "Harry?" She was still
holding the glass above her head.

Harry stood flat-footed and glared at the ground. A little drunkenly he swirled the ice in his glass.

After a few seconds of silence Mrs. Botkin coughed and
started toward the porch; the guests filed after her. Mildred
Apple was wearing white jersey. She got directly ahead of
Laura and walked as if she were about to start a hula.
Suzie and Tiny swung hands. Mr. Botkin, scowling,
brought up the rear.

During salad Laura Newton talked mostly to the people
on either side of Harry. Burgundy wine from France was
served with the steaks and while they were beginning on

that the sun went down. Then one by one the guests
stopped cutting their meat and looked through the porch
screen.

Fig Newton twisted the Phi Beta Kappa key on his chain
as he watched the condor lift first one foot and then the
other from its branch. Tiny Huddlestun leaned his ham-
bone elbows on the table and raised himself partly out of
his chair in order to see over Mrs. Botkin's fluffy white
head. Of the guests, only Harry Apple did not look; he
stared at his wine glass, turning it slowly with his fingers
on the stem. Mr. Botkin's eyes had narrowed in anticipa-
tion; he waited for the flight like an Occidental Buddha.

The condor's wings spread, brushing the leaves of other
branches, and at the size of the bird Laura dropped her
fork. Nobody picked it up, so it lay on the flagstones, its
tines sending out a persistent hum.

The black condor lifted its feet again. This caused the
chain which dangled from its neck to sway back and forth.

The dinner table was quiet. Only some June bugs fizzed
angrily as they tried to get through the screens.

Mildred Apple said abruptly, "I'm cold." Nobody
looked at her, so she went on in a sharp tone, "Why doesn't
somebody switch off that fan? I tell you I'm cold. I won't
sit here all night in a draft. I won't!"

Mr. Botkin did not turn his head, but growled, "Shut
up."

Mildred was shocked, but she recovered quickly. "Don't
you *dare* tell me to shut up! I won't stand for it! Do you
hear?" Mr. Botkin paid no attention to her, so she turned
petulantly to Harry; he was looking at his glass.

"Switch it off yourself," murmured Laura.

Mildred's eyes began to glitter. "I will not!"

"I'm ure nobody else is going to," Laura said in a dry voice.

Fig was getting ready to say something when Suzie Huddlestun gasped, "Oh!"

The condor took off so slowly that it did not seem real; it appeared only to be stretching, yet it was in the air. When its immense wings had spread and descended a second time its talons rose above the top branches, curling into metal-hard globes. For an instant the condor hung in the purple sky like an insignia of some great war plane, then its head was jerked down. It made its one sound, dropped to the warm ground, and lay without moving.

Laura Newton observed sourly, "What a simple bird." She looked across her tack-hammer nose at Harry.

Tiny grinned. "Now's the time to cook that turkey for Thanksgiving, Botkin." He looked all around the table but nobody chuckled and his eyes came back to Suzie. She laughed.

Fig took a sip of water and then cleared his throat. "Fowl," he said, after frowning in thought, "are not overly intelligent."

Twilight was ending. The guests could not see the condor distinctly, but only what looked like a gunny sack under the dying magnolia. Much later, while they were arguing bitterly over their bridge scores, they heard the condor's chain clinking and soon a branch creaked.

++

The Fisherman from Chihuahua

Santa Cruz is at the top of Monterey Bay, which is about
a hundred miles below San Francisco, and in the winter
there are not many people in Santa Cruz. The boardwalk
concessions are shuttered except for one counter-and-booth
restaurant, the Ferris-wheel seats are hooded with olive
green canvas and the powerhouse padlocked, and the
rococo doors of the carousel are boarded over and if one
peers through a knothole into its gloom the horses which
buck and plunge through summer prosperity seem like
animals touched by a magic wand that they may never
move again. Dust dims the gilt of their saddles and sifts
through cracks into their bold nostrils. About the only
sounds to be heard around the water front in Santa Cruz
during winter are the voices of Italian fishermen hidden
by mist as they work against the long pier, and the slap of
waves against the pilings of the cement dance pavilion
when tide runs high, or the squeak of a gull, or once in a
long time bootsteps on the slippery boards as some person
comes quite alone and usually slowly to the edge of the
gray and fogbound ocean.

The restaurant is Pendleton's and white brush strokes

55

on the glass announce *tacos, frijoles,* and *enchiladas* as
house specialties, these being mostly greens and beans and
fried meat made arrogant with pepper. Smaller letters in
pseudo-Gothic script say *Se Habla Espanol* but this is not
true; it was the man who owned the place before Pendleton who could speak Spanish. From him, though, Pendleton did learn how to make the food and this is the reason
a short fat Mexican who worked as a mechanic at Ace Dillon's Texaco station continued eating his suppers there.
He came in every night just after eight o'clock and sat at
the counter, ate an astounding amount of this food, which
he first splattered with tabasco sauce as casually as though
it were ketchup, and then washed it farther down with
beer. After that he would feel a little drunk and would
spend as much as two or even three dollars playing the
pinball machine and the great nickelodeon and dancing
by himself, but inoffensively, contentedly, just snapping
his fingers and shuffling across the warped boards often until Pendleton began pulling in the shutters. Then, having
had a suitable evening, he would half-dance his way home,
or at least back in the direction of town. He was a squat
little man who waddled like a duck full of eggs and he
had a face like a blunt arrowhead or a Toltec idol, and he
was about the color of hot sand. His fingers were much too
thick for their length, seemingly without joints, only
creases where it was necessary for them to bend. He
smelled principally of cold grease and of urine as though
his pants needed some air, but Pendleton who did not
smell very good himself did not mind and besides there
were not many customers during these winter months.

So every evening shortly after dark he entered for his
food and some amusement, and as he appeared to contain

all God's world within his own self Pendleton was not dis-
interested when another Mexican came in directly behind
him like a long shadow. This new man was tall, very tall,
possibly six feet or more, and much darker, almost black
in the manner of a sweat-stained saddle. He was handsome,
silent, and perhaps forty years of age. Also he was something of a dandy; his trousers, which were long and quite
tight, revealed the fact that he was bowlegged, as befits
certain types of men, and made one think of him easily
riding a large fast horse, not necessarily toward a woman
but in the direction of something more remote and mysterious—bearing a significant message or something like
that. Exceedingly short black boots of finest leather took
in his narrow trouser bottoms. For a shirt he wore long-
sleeved white silk unbuttoned to below the level of his
nipples which themselves were vaguely visible. The hair
of his chest was so luxuriant that an enameled crucifix
there did not even rest on the skin.

These two men sat at the counter side by side. The tall
one lifted off his sombrero as if afraid of mussing his hair
and he placed it on the third stool. His hair was deeply
oiled, and comb tracks went all the way from his temples
to the back of his thin black neck, and he gave out a scent
of green perfume. He had a mustache that consisted of
nothing but two black strings hanging across the corners
of his unforgiving mouth and ending in soft points about
an inch below his chin. He seemed to think himself alone
in the restaurant because, after slowly licking his lips and
interlacing his fingers, he just sat looking somberly ahead.
The small man ordered for them both.

After they had eaten supper the little one played the
pinball machine while this strange man took from his shirt

pocket a cigarillo only a little bigger than his mustache and smoked it with care; that is, he would take it from his mouth between his thumb and one finger as if he were afraid of crushing it, and after releasing the smoke he would replace it with the same care in the exact center of his mouth. It never dangled or rolled; he respected it. Nor was it a cheap piece of tobacco; its smoke ascended heavily, moist and sweet.

Suddenly the fat Mexican kicked the pinball game and with a surly expression walked over to drop a coin into the nickelodeon. The tall man had remained all this time at the counter with his long savage eyes half-shut, smoking and smoking the fragrant cigarillo. Now he did not turn around—in fact his single movement was to remove the stump from his lips—but clearly he was disturbed. When the music ended he sat totally motionless for several minutes. Then he lifted his head and his throat began to swell like that of a mating pigeon.

Pendleton, sponging an ash tray, staggered as if a knife had plunged through his ribs.

The Mexican's eyes were squeezed altogether shut. His lips had peeled back from his teeth like those of a jaguar tearing meat, and the veins of his neck looked ready to burst. In the shrill screams bursting from his throat was a memory of Moors, the ching of Arab cymbals, of rags and of running feet through all the market places of the East.

His song had no beginning; it had no end. All at once he was simply sitting on the stool looking miserably ahead.

After a while the small fat Mexican said to Pendleton "Be seeing you, man," and waddled through the door into darkness. A few seconds later the tall one's stool creaked. Without a sound he placed the high steepled sombrero like a crown on his hair and followed his friend through the door.

The next night there happened to be a pair of tourists eating in the back booth when the men entered. They were dressed as before except that the big one's shirt was lime green and Pendleton noticed his wrist watch, fastened not to his wrist actually but over the green cuff where it bulged like an oily bubble. They took the same stools and ate fried beans, tacos, and enchiladas for almost an hour, after which the short one who looked like his Toltec ancestors gently belched, smiled in a benign way, and moved over to his machine. Failing to win anything he cursed it and kicked it before selecting his favorite records.

This time Pendleton was alert; as the music ended he got ready for the first shriek. The tourists, caught unaware, thought their time had come. When they recovered from the shock they looked fearfully over the top of the booth and then the woman stood up in order to see better. After the black Mexican's song was finished they all could hear the incoming tide, washing softly around the pillars of the pavilion.

Presently the two men paid their bill and went out, the short one leading, into the dirty yellow fog and the diving, squeaking gulls.

"Why, that's terrible," the woman laughed. "It wasn't musical." Anyone who looked at her would know she was still shuddering from the force of the ominous man.

Her husband too was frightened and laughed. "Somebody should play a little drum behind that fellow." Unaware of what a peculiar statement he had made he formed a circle of his thumb and forefinger to show how big the drum should be.

She was watching the door, trying to frown compassionately. "I wonder what's the matter with that poor man. Some woman must have hurt him dreadfully."

Pendleton began to wipe beer bracelets and splats of tabasco sauce from the lacquered plywood counter where the men had been. The restaurant seemed too quiet.

The woman remarked cheerily, "We're from Iowa City."

Pendleton tried to think of something but he had never been to Iowa City or anywhere near it even on a train, so he asked if they would like more coffee.

The husband wondered, "Those two fellows, do they come in here every night?"

Pendleton was seized with contempt and hatred for this domestic little man, though he did not know why, and walked stiffly away from their booth without answering. He stood with both hairy hands on the shining urn while he listened to the sea thrashing and rolling under the night.

"Who?" he said gruffly. "Them two?"

A few minutes later while pouring coffee he said, "Sometimes I feel so miserable I could damn near roll up in a tube."

The couple, overpowered by his manner, looked up uneasily. The woman ventured, "It seems terribly lonely around here."

On the third evening as they seated themselves before the counter Pendleton said to the one who spoke American, "Tell your friend he can't yowl in here anymore."

"He's not my baby," this short fat man replied, not greatly interested. "Six tacos and four beers and a lot of beans."

"What do you think, I'm running a damn concert hall?"

For a moment the little Mexican became eloquent with his eyebrows; then both he and Pendleton turned their attention to the silent one who was staring somberly past the the case of pies.

Pendleton leaned on his hands so that his shoulders bulged. "Now looky, Pablo, give him the word and do it quick. Tell him to cut that noise out. You understand me?"

This enraged the small man whose voice rose to a snarl. "Pablo yourself. Don't give me that stuff."

Pendleton was not angry but set about cleaving greens for their tacos as though he were furious. While the blade chunked into the wood again and again beside his thumb he thought about the situation. He did not have anything particular in mind when all at once he banged down the cleaver and with teeth clenched began bending his eyes toward the two.

"No debe cantar," the little one said hurriedly, waggling a negative finger at his companion. No more singing. *"No mas."*

"That's better, by God," muttered Pendleton as though he understood. He wished to say something in Spanish about the matter but he knew only *mañana, adios,* and *señorita* and none of these seemed to fit. He resumed work, but doubtfully, not certain if the silent one had heard either of them. Over one shoulder he justified himself. "Folks come here to eat their suppers, not to hear any concert."

Abel W. Sharpe, who had once been the sheriff of Coda City and who now ripped tickets for a movie house on Pacific, came in the door alone but arguing harshly. The Toltec had started playing pinball so Sharpe took the vacant stool, looked up twice at the man beside him, and then dourly ordered waffles and hot milk. It was while he was pouring syrup into the milk that the nickelodeon music died and that the black Mexican did it again.

Pendleton was exasperated with himself for laughing and almost choked by trying to stop.

"Heh?" asked the old man, who at the first note had jumped off his stool and now crouched several feet away from the counter, a knife in one hand and his mug of sweet milk in the other. "I can't hear nothing. The bastard's deefened me."

The Toltec had not stopped playing pinball and paid none of them the least attention because he had lighted four pretty girls which meant he would probably win something. His friend now sat motionless on the stool and looked ahead as though he saw clear into some grief-stricken time.

Not until the eighth or maybe the ninth night did Pendleton realize that the restaurant was drawing more people; there would be six or eight or even as many as a dozen in for dinner.

There came a night when the fat Toltec entered as always but no one followed. That night the restaurant was an uneasy place. Things spilled, and while cleaning up one of the tables Pendleton discovered a menu burned through and through with cigarette holes. By ten-thirty the place was deserted.

Pendleton said, "Hey, Pablo."

The Toltec gave him a furious look.

"All right," Pendleton apologized, "what's your name?"

"What's yours?" he replied. He was deeply insulted.

"Whereabouts is your friend?"

"He's no friend of mine."

Pendleton walked down the counter behind a damp rag, wrung it over the sink, then very casually he did something he never did or never even thought of doing: he opened a bottle of beer for the Mexican and indicated without a word that it was free.

Toltec, though still grieved, accepted the gift, saying, "I just met the guy. He asked me where to get some decent cooking."

Pendleton wiped a table and for a time appeared to be idly picking his back teeth. When he judged the interval to be correct he asked, "Got tired of the grub here, I guess."

"No, tonight he's just drunk."

Pendleton allowed several more minutes, then, "He looks like a picture of a bullfighter I saw once in Tijuana called Victoriano Posada."

And this proved to be a shrewd inquiry because after drinking some more of the free beer the fat Mexican remarked, "He calls himself Damaso."

Pendleton, wondering if something else might follow, pretended to stretch and to yawn and smacked his chops mightily. He thought that tomorrow he would say, when the tall one entered, "Howdy, Damaso."

"Know what? He goes and stands by himself on the sea wall a lot of times. Maybe he's going to knock himself off. Wouldn't that be something?"

"Tell him not to do it in front of my place," Pendleton answered.

Through the screen door could be seen a roll of silvery yellow fog and above it the moon, but the water was hidden.

"These Santa Cruz winters," Pendleton said. Opening the icebox he selected a superior beer for himself and moved his high stool far enough away that his guest might not feel their friendship was being forced. Peeling off the wet label he rolled it into a soggy gray ball which he dropped into a bucket under the counter. "Singers make plenty money, I hear."

The Mexican looked at him slyly. "What are you talking about?"

Pendleton, scratching his head, sighed and yawned again. "Huh? Oh. I was just thinking about what's-his-name. That fellow you come in here with once or twice."

"I know it," the Mexican said, laughing.

For a while both of them drank away at their beers and listened to the combers, each of which sounded as if it would smash the door.

"Feels like there's something standing up in the ocean tonight," Pendleton said. "I could use a little summer."

"You want our beach full of tourists? Those sausages? Man, you're crazy. You're off the rocks."

Pendleton judged that the Mexican was about to insult the summer people still more, so he manipulated the conversation once again. "Somebody told me your friend got himself a singing job at that night spot near Capitola."

"Look," said the Toltec, patient, but irritated, "I just met the guy a couple of weeks ago."

"He never said where he's from, I guess."

"Chihuahua, he says. That's one rough town. And full of sand, Jesus Christ."

Breakers continued sounding just beyond the door and the fog now stood against the screen like a person.

"What does he do?"

The Mexican lifted both fat little shoulders.

"Just traveling through?"

The Mexican lifted both hands.

"Where is he going?"

"All I know is he's got a pretty good voice."

"He howls like a god-damn crazy wolf," Pendleton said, "howling for the moon."

"Yah, he's pretty good. Long time ago I saw a murder down south in the mountains and a woman screamed just like that."

Both of them thought about things, and Pendleton, having reflected on the brevity of human affairs and the futility of riches, opened his icebox for two more drinks. The Mexican accepted one as though in payment for service. For some seconds they had been able to hear footsteps approaching, audible after every tunnel of water caved in. The footsteps went past the door but no one could be seen.

"Know what? There was an old man washed up on the beach the other day."

"That so?" said Pendleton. "Everything gets to the beach sooner or later."

The Mexican nodded. Somewhere far out on the bay a little boat sounded again and again. "What a night," he said.

Pendleton murmured and scratched.

"Know something, mister?"

Pendleton, now printing wet circles on his side of the counter, asked what that might be.

"Damaso is no Mexicano."

"I didn't think so," Pendleton lied.

"No, because he's got old blood. You know what I mean? I think he's a gypsy from Spain, or wherever those guys come from. He's dark in the wrong way. He just don't *feel* Mexicano to me. There's something about him, and besides he speaks a little Castellano."

Both of them considered all this.

"I suppose he's howling about some girl."

"No, it's bigger than that."

"What's the sound say?"

But here the little Mexican lost interest; he revolved on the stool, from which only his toes could reach to the floor, hopped off, and hurried across to the nickelodeon. Having pushed a nickel through the slit he studied the wonderful colors and followed the bubbles which fluttered up the tubes to vanish; next he dialed *"The Great Speckled Bird"* and began shuffling around the floor, snapping his fingers and undulating so that in certain positions he looked about five months pregnant.

"Who knows?" he asked of no one in particular while he danced.

The next night also he entered alone. When Pendleton mentioned this he replied the dark one was still drunk.

And the next night when asked if the drunk was going into its third day he replied that Damaso was no longer drunk, just sick from being so, that he was at present lying on the wet cement having vomited on his boots, that probably by sunrise he would be all right. This turned out to be correct because both of them came in for supper the following night. Toltec, smiling and tugging at his crotch, was rumpled as usual and smelled human while his tall companion was oiled and groomed and wearing the white silk again. A good many people were loitering about the restaurant—every booth was full—because this thing had come to be expected, and though all of them were eating or drinking or spending money in some way to justify themselves, and although no one looked up at the entrance of the two Mexicans there could be no doubt about the situation. Only these two men seemed not to notice anything; they ate voraciously and drank a lot of beer after which the one went across to his game, which had been deliberately vacated, and Damaso remained on the stool with his long arms crossed on the counter.

Later the nickelodeon lighted up. When at last its music died and the table stopped there was not a sound in all the restaurant. People watched the head of the dark man bow down until it was hidden in his arms. The crucifix disentangled itself and dropped out the top of his gaucho shirt where it began to swing to and fro, glittering as it twisted on the end of its golden chain. He remained like that for almost an hour, finally raised his head to look at the ticket, counted away enough money, and with the sombrero loosely in one hand he stumbled out the door.

The other Mexican paid no attention; he called for more beer, which he drank all at once in an attempt to interest a young girl with silver slippers and breasts like pears who was eating supper with her parents, but, failing to win anything at this or again at the machine, he suddenly grew bored with the evening and walked out.

The next night he entered alone. When asked if his companion had started another drunk he said Damaso was gone.

Pendleton asked late in the evening, "How do you know?"

"I feel it," he said.

Big Pendleton then stood listening to the advancing tide which had begun to pat the pillars like someone gently slapping a dead drum. After taking off his apron he rolled it tight, as he always did, and put it beneath the counter. With slow fingers he untied the sweaty handkerchief from around his neck and folded it over the apron, but there his routine altered; before pulling in shutters he stood a while beside the screen and looked out and listened, but of course received no more than he expected, which was fog, the sound of the sea, and its odor.

Sharply the Toltec said, "I like to dance." And he began to do so. "Next summer I'm really going to cut it up. Nothing's going to catch me." He read Pendleton's face while dancing by himself to the odd and clumsy little step he was inventing, and counseled, "Jesus Christ, he's gone. Forget about it, man."

I'll Take You to Tennessee

Logos Jackson's grin kept on growing until it almost slid off his face. "Sure," he said, "sure we can have a picnic." He unwrapped his big bony hands from the pump handle and grabbed Roy and Dutch-rubbed him, and all the kids piled onto Logos, laughing and shouting. And all the while Logos kept grunting and grabbing an arm or a leg and threatening to have them all thrown in jail for picking on him.

"Picnics—" said Logos, "—ugly kids!" He stood up, shaking them off. "Go on. Go away."

"Come on, Logos! You said you would—you said you would!"

Logos wagged his head, but then the grin crept back. "Eleven o'clock," he said. "Now get. I got work to do."

Roy was the first to get back to the shed where Logos lived with his three Tennessee hound-dogs. Roy got there just before ten-thirty. He hugged the two-by-four that propped up the porch and yelled for Logos to come out, but Logos didn't answer. The other kids got there pretty soon and they all yelled and banged on the door so much that finally the door opened a crack and Logos's big hand shot out and grabbed Boulton Polk by the britches. Everybody yelled and jumped off the porch while Boulton screamed as he was dragged inside. Everything was quiet. But then Luanne giggled, so they all ran up on the porch again and began to beat on the old plank door.

Logos poked his head out and the crooked scar around his neck stretched. He blinked like one of the possums he was always telling them about. "What you all want?" he asked. He saw Maxine Crowe standing in back of the gang. Maxine was almost sixteen. She wore sandals and a dress with a Mexican belt.

"Picnic! Picnic! Come on, Logos, you said you would!"

"Picnic?" said Logos. He sneaked out a long stringy arm and grabbed Betty Su by the ear, and Boulton wiggled out through the door. "What picnic?"

But they all yelled again and poured in to rescue Betty Su, and Bert Rice announced he was going to pry off the hinges of the door with his sheath knife, so finally Logos turned her ear loose. "Come on," he said. "Perch ain't going to bite all day." He lifted the rust-covered shovel from behind the door and ambled out of his shed to the dumping ground.

"Naw," he complained, "dismals come back. Can't go. All wore out." He stuck the shovel in the ground and reached down to lace his white canvas sneakers.

"Worms!" shouted Roy. He grabbed onto Logos's belt and tried to swing from it. "Worms, worms, worms, worms—"

"Yeah, get us some bait, Logos!"

"Yeah!" And Georgia Lee Small hopped around, hitting Logos in the ribs and back. "Yeah, yeah, yeah—"

So Logos grinned again, showing his good teeth, and

without saying anything else he began to spade up the dump for worms.

Logos had been born in Tennessee, way up near Three-Forks-of-the-Wolf, he used to say, way high in the Tennessee mountains. He'd been raised there. He'd worked a little place, but it was so rocky that the crops wouldn't grow much, so one day Logos had just called his hound-dogs together and they'd walked south and west until the rocks and the hills and the lightning storms had drifted back out of sight. They'd walked to the edge of a plain where there were farms, cut through with creeks and hollows, and a river and a town. There the sun was a long way off. Logos had stopped. That had been eight years ago. He was forty-three now; two of his hounds were buried behind the shed.

Usually in the afternoons, when the sun had cooled and the tree locusts were scratching, the kids would straggle over to Logos's place for a story about Tennessee. They'd squat and sprawl in the dust in front of his porch, sharpening their pocket knives on their pants, or frogging each other on the arm while Logos leaned back against the two-by-four and settled himself. When he'd begin to talk, the boys would stop pretending there weren't any girls in the gang and they'd all fall quiet, listening. He'd lean against the timber on his rickety porch and squint out into the red sun, like he was remembering a million years ago, and he'd tell stories in his Tennessee voice that somehow hadn't ever learned that folks don't care much about the handyman in a dusty little southern town.

He'd tell about the gimpy nigger who'd worked the place in back of his, and the Pentecostal baptisms in the river with the preachers spelling each other sometimes, yelling and ducking the sinners. He'd talk about sitting on a hilltop at night, listening to the dogs chase a fox over the ridges. Sometimes he'd talk about how lightning broke in the hills, or how everybody tried to raise a good mule. A good mule would bring three or even four hundred dollars, Logos said.

Evered Evans liked to hear about the tobacco barns, so almost every evening Logos would have to tell him about the hickory fire leaking smoke through the cracks in the roof. Boulton Polk wanted to hear about the smokehouse and how side meat was hung. Ella wanted to hear how potatoes were heled in and dug up when winter came.

"Tell us about the trees," would say Luanne. "How do the trees feel when you touch them?"

So Logos would have to tell her all over again about the white oaks and the gray cedars, or the dogwoods with their rough checkery bark. And to the gang it seemed as though Logos Jackson was at least a million years old. They'd tell him he was a million, but he would just laugh. "I'll take you all to Tennessee someday," he'd say.

The rusty shovel glinted once or twice in the sun as Logos spaded up the dump. The sweat began to smell and his blue shirt with the sleeves cut off got limp. He'd turn up a spadeful of the dump and Roy and Boulton Polk would each jump for it, pulling out the worms and dropping them into the can.

"We got sixteen," whispered Betty Su.

"I can't put worms on the hook," said Luanne.

"Logos, why do we have to take girls on the picnic anyway?" asked Sidney Thomas.

"Got to like girls," said Logos without looking up.

Maxine smiled. "Why?"

He wiped the sweat from his mouth and chuckled. "Account of you came from my rib, honey. We're all God's children."

"We only got sixteen worms still," said Roy. "Get some more."

Maxine played with her hair. "Don't you like me, Logos?"

"Sure, I like you. Like all you kids—all you ugly kids."

"I don't mean that. I've grown up. I'm a woman."

Logos turned to his shovel. Maxine watched the muscles of his shoulders bunch and slide under the wet shirt.

Boulton Polk looked up from the worms. "Phooey!" he said.

"How many we got?"

"How many we got, Betty Su?"

"Twenty-three," answered Roy.

"That's enough."

Georgia Lee wiped her hands on her jeans. She grabbed for the can. "Let me carry them."

"You'll spill them," decided Sidney. "I'll carry them. Girls always spill things." He pushed a worm back.

"I get to carry them part way," said Boulton.

Logos stuck his shovel in the dirt and grinned.

Georgia Lee wiped her hands again and looked at the can and then at Sidney. Logos headed the gang toward the path that zigged through the dirty brown weeds.

"Are we going to catch perch today, Logos?"

"I brought a sandwich, Logos."

"What part of the creek are we going to, Logos?"

"That's no way to string a worm." Logos took Luanne's hook in a hand that was almost as hard as the barb. He threaded the worm and dropped the line into the sunny pool. Luanne studied the cork. She crouched on the bank with tense wrists.

"Now you let him get a hold before you jerk him out of there."

Luanne nodded quickly, never raising her eyes from the cork.

Roy plowed through the briar patch. "I got one, Logos! I got one! I got one!"

Logos inspected the catch. "Throw him back. Too small to eat."

Roy unhooked the tiny perch and laid it carefully in the shallows. "Whillickers!" he said.

"Logos, will you put on my worm?" Maxine seated herself on a log where she could watch as Logos adjusted her tackle. "I hate worms. They're so slimy."

Logos grinned down at her. His hands moved quickly, the fingers throwing shadows. Maxine watched. Her wide mouth smiled, thanking him.

"Lay off that fire, Mr. Polk. Cooking fire's small." Logos reached into the can for another worm. "You catch us a mess of fish. I'll fix that fire." He handed a line to Boulton and pulled a stick from the fire.

Maxine's hand closed over Logos's on the stick. "I'll fix it. I don't care about fishing." Then she said to Boulton, "Go on. You heard what Logos said." She stooped and poked at the blaze, moving her knees away from the heat.

Luanne jumped back, whirling her bamboo stick. "Logos!" she shrieked, and ran to bend over the sunfish flopping on the bank.

"That's not so big," observed Sidney. "I've caught bigger ones than that."

Ella poked interestedly.

Maxine spoke. "Kill it."

They all turned around and looked at her.

"Hit it on the head." She rocked forward. "Or do you want to eat it alive?" She tossed a branch toward the group.

Sidney picked up the branch and looked down at the little fish, squirming in the dust and dry beard grass. He shifted the branch to his other hand and doubled up his fist.

"Well," said Maxine, "go ahead. Smack it."

Sidney spit on the ground and mashed his toe in the spit. "I will," he said. "I will okay."

She stood up, placing her palms deliberately on her angular hips.

Sidney mashed the spit again. He dropped to his knees and took hold of the fishing line. The fish wriggled. Sidney put down his branch. "He threw water in my eyes. I can't see."

"Kill it!"

"Well—*you* kill him."

Maxine picked up the branch and stunned the fish. She ripped the hook from its mouth, and turned to find Logos staring at her.

Evered Evans came around the bend with a turtle. Bert showed up with a perch and another one that Logos said was diseased. Georgia Lee didn't catch anything, but Logos told her that if it hadn't been for her sandwich they couldn't have cooked the fish with bread crumbs. The fish were just right.

After dinner Roy asked for a story.

Logos poked at the fire and grinned and said he didn't

know any more stories, but Roy grabbed his wrist and curled up his knees and said he wasn't ever going to let go until Logos told a story. So Logos said all right because he sure didn't want such a dumb ugly little roughneck swinging on his arm all the rest of his life. He sat down on a patch of turkeyfoot and told the gang to get settled because they were making too much rumpus. They spraddled out flat around him, mostly on their stomachs with their chins in their hands, except Maxine. She walked across from where Logos was facing and sat on a log and drew up her legs to get more comfortable.

Logos started off by saying he was so old that when he was born his mother couldn't think of anything to name him, because way back then nobody had names. All the gang laughed except Maxine. She smiled and leaned on her hands. She asked Logos how old he was. Logos looked up, but he couldn't see her face behind the fire. He rubbed his long thin nose. Then he grabbed a chip of wood and tossed it at her and the kids laughed again, only Maxine took the chip and dropped it down the front of her blouse. Logos looked into the fire for a minute and broke a stick, but finally he went on talking. He told all about a fox hunt, the best fox hunt they'd ever had in the Tennessee hills, and how when they skinned the fox he was eleven feet long.

Maxine leaned back on her hands again. When the kids had stopped yelling and booing she said she wished she could find a man that big. She ran her tongue over her upper lip and sucked in her breath until the blouse stretched tight. Logos went on talking, only sometimes his stories wandered. Roy asked him what was the matter.

Bert and Evered whittled. "How big is the jockey yard?" asked Evered.

"Tell me about Mule Day in Columbia," whispered Betty Su. She sat with her ankles crossed under her in the dust. Her solemn gray eyes seemed even bigger behind the thick glasses. "Do the ladies really ride the mules in the parade? Do they ride the real mules?"

Logos pushed a finger down inside one of his sneakers and popped out a twig. Then he told how the pretty girls jumped on the jackasses and rode in the big parade when Columbia had Mule Day back east in Tennessee.

"Tell me about the revivals in the strawpens and the cunjur doctors."

So Logos told Ella about the revival meetings back in the hill country, about the niggers getting baptized; and why you should always plant a garden in the full of the moon.

"How do I catch a husband, Logos?" asked Maxine.

Logos grinned and spit through his teeth. "First day of May hold a mirror over a well."

Maxine smiled, tangling her hair with one finger. "I'm grown up. I don't want to wait on my honeymoon that long."

Logos tried to grin again. "Sleep with a beef bone under your pillow—" He threw another stick of wood at the fire.

"Aw, whillickers! Cut out that mush. What's a cunjur doctor, Logos?"

Then Logos told about the cunjur doctors selling "hands" and "tobies" to the niggers to ward off spells and to catch witches.

"What about the cunjur doctor with the three birth-marks on his arm?"

"Father and Son and Holy Ghost," Logos answered, but he didn't seem very interested in telling stories any more.

"I got a wart," announced Georgia Lee.

"Black calf lick it three times on three days."

"What do they do in the revivals, Logos?"

"Oh, jump, roll around, wrestle with the Devil," he answered, poking at the fire.

Luanne cried happily,

> "I'll tell you who the Lord loves best—
> It's the shouting Methodist!"

And Roy countered,

> "Baptist, Baptist, Baptist—
> Baptist till I die.
> I'll go along with the Baptists
> And find myself on high!

Isn't that right, Logos?"

"Do you go to church, Logos?" asked Maxine.

"They don't have his church here," said Evered.

"I belong to all churches that knows the Word of God," he answered.

Maxine slipped off her sandals and squeezed dust between her toes.

"Maxine's got a dimple in her knee! What does that mean?"

Logos chuckled and his good white teeth showed again. "Means there's the Devil in her," he said. But nobody laughed.

The sun was going down. Maxine ran her tongue over her lips and rubbed the outside of her thin thighs. She looked at Logos across the firelight. She turned around to look at the sun, and the fire reflected the color in her hair.

"Maxine's got pretty hair," said Roy, "for a girl."

Evered snorted and looked sideways at Bert.

Maxine stood up in back of the log. She stretched her arms until her blouse pulled tight again. "I've lost my fishing tackle. Don't you reckon I better find it before it gets dark?"

Logos didn't say anything.

"I can't recollect exactly where it is. Maybe—you better come along. I might get lost."

"You can find it."

"All right," said Maxine. She eased her palms down over the bones of her hips. She opened her mouth to say something, but then just licked her teeth. "All right," she said at last. She left her sandals on the log and turned and wandered off into the darkening hollow.

"She didn't lose no old fishing tackle. She didn't even go fishing. She said worms are slimy." Sidney appealed to Logos for confirmation.

"Maxine Crowe," said Roy. "Ugh! Maxine Scarecrow."

"She sure has got pretty hair," said Bert. He glanced over at Evered.

Sidney pulled up his socks. "I don't like her."

"Neither do I," said Ella.

"She is a lamb lost in the wilderness," murmured Logos into the fire.

Night drifted in over the farmlands and the smoke faded from black to gray-blue. Beyond Jess Phillips' land the weak yellow lights of the town popped through the darkness, one by one. A breeze sneaked across the creek and wiggled the smoke, but there weren't many leaves to rustle. Down the field an owl screamed and a dog barked. A train whistled over somewhere near the sun. A mouse ticked a dry branch, and the sky changed from red to purple and finally died.

"Sing us a song, Logos."

So Logos hummed for a while, and sang words, but they weren't connected.

When he had finished the gang didn't talk. Bert remembered to pick up the stick he had been whittling on, but he didn't cut any more. He laid it down softly.

The night was quiet; the fire didn't crackle very loud.

"Reckon I better go find her," said Logos at last. "She's been gone a long time." He roughed Roy's head and stepped over Ella and wandered off toward the dark hollow.

"Maxine!" they heard him call, and heard it drift with the wind. "Maxine, honey!"

A star began to shine over in the east just above the briar, but there weren't any other lights. A branch snapped down in the hollow and another dog barked way off over the black fields, and then they couldn't hear any more.

"Whillickers!" said Roy sleepily. "He's been gone a long time."

"Yeah."

"Think we ought to go after him?"

"No," said Evered. "We'd just all get scattered out. We better wait."

Ella and Betty Su and Luanne sat close together. "Put some sticks on," said Betty Su.

"You're afraid of the dark," said Sidney disgustedly.

"So are you."

"I am not!"

"Are so!"

"The moon's coming up—"

"Shh!"

"What's the matter?" hissed Ella.

"Shh!" Bert peered into the night. "No, I guess it's nothing."

"What did you hear?"

"Nothing. I thought I heard them."

"Put some more sticks on."

Roy pulled out his knife and thumbed the edge. "I bet this is the sharpest old knife in the world." He jabbed at the ground, popping up little chunks of dirt.

"I had a knife sharper than that once."

"You did not."

"Did so!"

"Shh—"

"Are they coming?"

"Can you hear them, Bert?"

"I don't know. There's something." Bert stood up. "Push that big branch on." He walked to the edge of the circle of light and squinted toward the hollow. "Logos! Hey, Logos! Is that you?"

Evered stood up. "Hey, Logos!"

Luanne bit her lip. "I don't think he's ever going to come back." She coughed and ground her fists in her eyes. The owl screamed again and she took Betty Su's hand. "He's not ever going to come back."

"Oh, cut it out." Boulton stood on the log, smacking his fist into the palm of his other hand.

Luanne began to sniffle. "No, he's not. Something's happened."

Roy sat staring into the coals with his knife balanced on one knee.

"Poke it up."

"Oh, who's cold?"

"I'm not, but poke it up anyway. I can't see."

Roy pushed a branch farther in with the blade of his knife. He rubbed his forehead.

Bert ran out into the night. "Logos! Yea, Logos!"

Luanne and Georgia Lee jumped up and stared into the dark. "Logos?" called Georgia Lee.

Maxine walked into the light of the fire. She was crying. Logos followed her in. He carried his blue shirt in one hand.

"Hey, Logos," exclaimed Evered, "we thought you'd got lost yourself!"

"I have lost myself, boy."

"Gee, Logos, what's the matter? You look funny."

"Put on your sweater, boy. You all pack up."

Luanne began to cry.

They collected their pocket knives and their shoes and their rubber gun pistols in silence. Logos stood by the fire with his eyes closed, the red light of the flames deepening the scar around his neck.

"I guess that's everything," said Bert.

Logos scattered the sticks of the fire and walked heavily on the embers until there was just moonlight.

"You didn't even go fishing!" blurted Roy. He turned around and kicked at Maxine's sandals.

Maxine put her fingers in her mouth.

They all went home. Logos opened a can and ate. Then he filled his pockets and called his hound-dogs and started walking.

The Walls of Ávila

Thou shalt make castels in Spayne,
And dreme of joye, al but in vayne.
—ROMAUNT OF THE ROSE

Ávila lies only a few kilometers west and a little north of
Madrid, and is surrounded by a grim stone wall that was
old when Isabella was born. Life in this town has not
changed very much from the days when the earth was flat;
somehow it is as though news of the passing centuries has
never arrived in Ávila. Up the cobbled street saunters a
donkey with a wicker basket slung on each flank, and on
the donkey's bony rump sits a boy nodding drowsily in the
early morning sun. The boy's dark face looks medieval. He
is delivering bread. At night the stars are metallic, with a
bluish tint, and the Spaniards stroll gravely back and forth
beside the high stone wall. There are not so many gypsies,
or *gitanos,* in this town as there are in, say, Valencia or
Seville. Ávila is northerly and was not impressed by these
passionate Asiatic people, at least not the way Córdoba
was, or Granada.

These were things we learned about Ávila when J. D. returned. He came home after living abroad for almost ten
years. He was thinner and taller than any of us remembered, and his crew-cut hair had turned completely gray
although he was just thirty-eight. It made him look very
distinguished, even a little dramatic. His skin was now as
brown as coffee, and there were wind wrinkles about his
restless cerulean blue eyes, as though the light of strange
beaches and exotic plazas had stamped him like a visa to
prove he had been there. He smiled a good deal, perhaps
because he did not feel at ease with his old friends any
more. Ten years did not seem long to us, not really long,
and we were disconcerted by the great change in him.
Only his voice was familiar. At the bus station where three
of us had gone to meet him only Dave Zobrowski recognized him.

Apparently this town of Ávila meant a great deal to
J. D., although he could not get across to us its significance.
He said that one night he was surprised to hear music and
laughter coming from outside the walls, so he hurried
through the nearest gate, which was set between two gigantic watch towers, and followed the wall around until
he came to a carnival. There were concessions where you
could fire corks at cardboard boxes, each containing a
chocolate bar, or dip for celluloid fishes with numbered
bellies, and naturally there was a carousel, the same as in
America. It rotated quite slowly, he said, with mirrors
flashing from its peak while enameled stallions gracefully
rose and descended on their gilded poles. But nothing was
so well attended as a curious swing in which two people
stood, facing each other, grasping a handle, and propelled
themselves so high that at the summit they were nearly

upside down. The shadow of this swing raced up the wall and down again. "Like this!" J. D. exclaimed, gesturing, and he stared at each of us in turn to see if we understood. He said it was like the shadow of some grotesque instrument from the days of the Inquisition, and he insisted that if you gazed up into the darkness long enough you could make out, among the serrated ramparts of the ancient wall, the forms of helmeted men leaning on pikes and gazing somberly down while their black beards moved in the night wind.

He had tales of the Casbah in Tangiers and he had souvenirs from the ruins of Carthage. On his key chain was a fragment of polished stone, drilled through the center, that he had picked up from the hillside just beyond Tunis. And he spoke familiarly of the beauty of Istanbul, and of Giotto's tower, and the Seine, and the golden doors of Ghiberti. He explained how the Portuguese are fuller through the cheeks than are the Spaniards, their eyes more indolent and mischievous, and how their songs—*fados,* he called them—were no more than lazy cousins of the fierce flamenco one heard throughout Andalusia.

When Zobrowski asked in what year the walls of Ávila were built J. D. thought for quite a while, his lean face sober while he gently rocked a tumbler of iced rum, but at last he said the fortifications were probably begun seven or eight hundred years ago. They had been repaired occasionally and were still impregnable to primitive force. It was queer, he added, to come upon such a place, indestructible when assaulted on its own terms, yet obsolete.

He had postal cards of things that had interested him. He had not carried a camera because he thought it bad manners. We did not completely understand what he meant by this but we had no time to discuss it because he was running on, wanting to know if we were familiar with Giambologna, saying, as he displayed a card, "In a grotto of the Boboli Gardens not far from the Uffizi—" He stopped abruptly. It had occurred to him that we might be embarrassed. No one said anything. None of us had ever heard of the Boboli Gardens, or of the sculptor Giambologna, or of the Venus that J. D. had wanted to describe.

"Here's the Sistine Chapel, of course," he said, taking another card from his envelope. "That's the Libyan sybil."

"Yes," said Zobrowski. "I remember this. There was a print of it in one of our high-school textbooks. Good God, how time does pass."

"Those damn textbooks," J. D. answered. "They ruin everything. They've ruined Shakespeare and the Acropolis and half the things on earth that are really worth seeing. Just like the Lord's Prayer—I can't hear it. I don't know what it says. Why wasn't I left to discover it for myself? Or the Venus de Milo. I sat in front of it for an hour but I couldn't see it."

He brought out a postal card of a church tower. At the apex was a snail-like structure covered with what appeared to be huge tile baseballs.

"That's the *Sagrada Familia*," he explained. "It's not far from the bull ring in Barcelona."

The *Sagrada Familia* was unfinished; in fact it consisted of nothing but a façade with four tremendous towers rising far above the apartment buildings surrounding it. He said it was a landmark of Barcelona, that if you should get lost in the city you had only to get to a clearing and look around for this weird church. On the front of it was a cement Christmas tree, painted green and hung with cement ornaments, while the tiled spires were purple and yellow. And down each spire ran vertical lettering that could be read a kilometer away. Zobrowski asked what was written on the towers.

"There's one word on each tower," said J. D. "The only one I recall is 'Ecstasy.'"

Dave Zobrowski listened with a patient, critical air, as though wondering how a man could spend ten years in such idle traveling. Russ Lyman, who had once been J. D.'s closest friend, listened in silence with his head bowed. When we were children together it had been Russ who intended to go around the world some day, but he had not, for a number of reasons. He seemed to hold a monopoly on bad luck. The girl he loved married somebody else, then his business failed, and so on and on through the years. Now he worked as a drugstore clerk and invested his pitiful savings in gold mines or wildcat oil wells. He had been thirty-two when the girl he loved told him good-by, tapping the ash from her cigarette onto his wrist to emphasize that she meant it; he promptly got drunk, because he could not imagine anything else to do, and a few days later he began going around with a stout, amiable girl named Eunice who had grown up on a nearby farm. One October day when the two of them were walking through an abandoned orchard they paused to rest in the shade of an old stone wall in which some ivy and small flowers were growing. Eunice was full of the delicate awkwardness of certain large girls, and while Russell was looking at her a leaf came fluttering down to rest on her shoulder. He became aware of the sound of honeybees flickering through the noonday sun, and of the uncommonly sweet odor of apples moldering among the clover, and he was seized with such passion that he immediately took the willing girl. She became pregnant, so they got married, although he did not want to, and before much longer he stopped talking about going around the world.

J. D., handing Russell a card of a little street in some North African town, remarked that on this particular street he had bought a tasseled red fez. And Russell nodded a bit sadly.

"Now, this is Lisbon," J. D. said. "Right over here on the far side of this rectangular plaza is where I lived. I used to walk down to the river that you see at the edge of the card, and on the way back I'd wander through some little shops where you can buy miniature galleons of filigreed gold."

"I suppose you bought one," said Zobrowski.

"I couldn't resist," said J. D. with a smile. "Here's a view of Barcelona at night, and right here by this statue of Columbus I liked to sit and watch the tide come sweeping in. An exact copy of the *Santa Maria* is tied up at the dock near the statue. And whenever the wind blew down from the hills I could hear the butter-pat clap of the gypsies dancing on the Ramblas." He looked at us anxiously to see if we were interested. It was clear that he loved Spain. He wanted us to love it, too.

"One time in Galicia," he said, "at some little town where the train stopped I bought a drink of water from a wrinkled old woman who was holding up an earthen jug and calling, '*Agua! Agua fria!*'" He drew a picture of the jug—it was called a *porrón*—and he demonstrated how it was to be held above your head while you drank. Your lips were never supposed to touch the spout. The Spaniards could drink without swallowing, simply letting the stream

of water pour down their throats, and after much drib-
bling and choking J. D. had learned the trick. But what he
most wanted to describe was the old woman who sold him
the water. She could have been sixty or ninety. She was
toothless, barefoot, and with a rank odor, but somehow,
in some way he could not get across to us, they had meant
a great deal to each other. He tried to depict a quality of
arrogance or ferocity about her, which, in the days when
she was young, must have caused old men to murmur and
young men to fall silent whenever she passed by. He could
not forget an instant when he reached out the train window to give her back the clay jug and met her deep, un-
wavering eyes.

"The train was leaving," he said, leaning forward. "It
was leaving forever. And I heard her scream at me. I didn't
know what she said, but there was a Spaniard in the same
compartment who told me that this old Galician woman
had screamed at me, 'Get off the train! Stay in my land!'"
He paused, apparently remembering, and slowly shook his
head.

It was in Spain, too, in a cheap water-front night club
called *El Hidalgo*—and he answered Russell's question by
saying that Don Quixote, for example, was an *hidalgo*—it
was here that he fell in love for the only time in his life.
The cabaret was in an alley of the Gothic quarter where
tourists seldom ventured. J. D. often spent his evenings
there, buying lottery tickets and brown paper cigarettes
and drinking a yellowish wine called *manzanilla*. One
night the flamenco dancers were in a furious mood—he
said he could feel the tension gathering the way electricity
will sometimes gather on a midwestern afternoon until it
splits the air. An enormously fat gypsy woman was dancing

by herself, dancing the symbols of fertility that have sur-
vived a thousand generations. She was dressed in what he
likened to a bedspread covered with orange polka dots.
Raising and lowering her vast arms she snapped her fingers
and angrily danced alone; then all at once a savage little
man in high-heeled boots sprang out of the crowd and began leaping around her. The staccato of his boots made the
floor tremble and caused the manzanilla to sway inside the
bottles.

"Everybody was howling and clapping," said J. D., and
he clapped once as the gypsies clap, not with the entire
hand but with three fingers flat against the palm. It
sounded like a pistol shot. "Somebody was looking at me,"
he went on. "I could feel someone's eyes on me. I looked
into the shadows and saw her. She was about nineteen, very
tall and imperial, with her hair in braids. She began walking toward me, and she was singing. She sang to me that
her name was Paquita—"

"She was improvising a song," said Zobrowski.

J. D. nodded. "It had the sound of a lament. Those old
tragedies you hear in Spain, they're paralyzing."

"Just what do you mean?" Zobrowski asked.

"I don't know," said J. D. "It's as if a dagger was still
plunged to the hilt in her breast."

Zobrowski smiled. "Go on. No doubt this young woman
was beautiful."

"Yes. And she never stopped looking at me. I don't remember what happened, but she must have walked across
the room because I realized I was standing up and she was
standing directly in front of me, touching my lips with one
finger."

"I have had similar dreams," said Zobrowski.

Russell was listening avidly. "I didn't think Spanish women could ever get away from their chaperons."

"*Dueña,* I believe, is the word," Zobrowski said.

"There was no *dueña* for that girl," answered J. D. He was silent for a little while and then concluded his story. "Later that night I saw her walking the streets."

"Well, that explains everything," Zobrowski smiled. "You simply mistook her professional interest in you for some sort of transcendental love."

J. D. looked at Dave Zobrowski for a long time, and finally said, "I didn't think I could make you understand." To Russell he said, "I find myself repeating her name. In the night I see her everywhere. In Paris, or in Rome, or even in this town, I see a girl turning away and my heart hesitates as it did that night in Barcelona."

"You should have married her," said Russell.

"I think he has done enough foolish things as it is," Zobrowski replied, and that seemed to end the matter. At least J. D. never referred to Paquita again. He spoke of the Andalusian gypsies, saying that they are a mixture of Arab and Indian, while the Catalonians are almost pure Sudra Indian. He gave this information as though it were important; he seemed to value knowledge for itself alone. But, looking into our faces, he saw that we could not greatly care about Spanish gypsies one way or another.

He had a pale gray cardboard folder with a drawing of St. George on the cover. Inside was a map of the geographical limits of the Catalan language, and this inscription: "With the best wishes for all the friends of the Catalan speaking countries once free in the past they will be free and whole again thanks to the will and strength of the Catalan people."

This was a folder of the resistance movement; it had been given to him, at the risk of imprisonment and perhaps at the risk of life itself, by a charwoman of Valencia. Zobrowski inquired if these were the people who opposed Franco. J. D. said that was correct. In Algiers he had met a waiter who had fought against Franco and barely escaped the country; this waiter had been in Algiers since 1938 and had no hope of seeing his family again, though he believed, as the charwoman believed, that one day Spain would be free.

After inspecting the pathetic little folder Zobrowski suggested, "I can easily appreciate your concern for these people. However you might also spend some time considering your own situation. Frankly, time is getting on, while you elect to dawdle about the water fronts of the world."

J. D. shrugged.

"I've been meaning to ask," said Zobrowski. "Did you ever receive the letter I addressed to you in Vienna?"

"I don't remember it," said J. D.

"It concerned an executive position with the Pratt Hanover Company. They manufacture farm implements. I spoke to Donald Pratt about you and he was very much interested."

"No, I never got the letter," said J. D. and he grinned. "I was traveling quite a bit and I guess a lot of letters never caught up with me."

"Would you have come back if you had received the offer from Pratt?"

"No, I guess not," said J. D., rather apologetically.

"We've known each other a long time, haven't we?"

J. D. nodded. "Since we were kids, Dave."

"Exactly. I would like to know how you manage to live."

"Oh, I work here and there. I had a job at the American embassy in Switzerland for a while, and to be honest about it, I've done some black marketing. I've learned how to get along, how to pull the levers that operate the world."

Then he began to describe Lucerne. It seemed far distant, in every dimension, from the days when we were children and used to bicycle down the river road to the hickory woods and hunt for squirrels. Each of us had a .22 rifle, except J. D., who went hunting with a lemonwood bow. He had made it himself, and he had braided and waxed the string, and sewn a quiver, and planed his arrows. He did not hit many squirrels with his equipment, and we would often taunt him about losing the arrows among the high weeds and underbrush, but he never seemed to mind; he would go home to his father's tool chest in the basement and calmly set about planing another batch of sticks. We would watch him clip turkey feathers into crisp rhomboids and carefully glue them into place, bracing each feather with matchsticks until the glue hardened. We would sit on the wash tub, or on his father's work bench, and smoke pieces of grapevine while we studied the new arrows. When he fitted on the bronze tip and banded each arrow with hunter's green and white Russell would watch with an almost hypnotized expression. But Dave Zobrowski, even in those days, was puzzled and a trifle impatient with J. D.

Remembering such things as J. D.'s bow and arrow we could see that it was he, and not Russell, who was destined to go away. We thought he had left a good deal of value here in the midwest of America. Our town is not exotic, but it is comprehensible and it is clean. This is partly due to Dave Zobrowski, who has always been vehement about cleanliness. That he grew up to become a physician and a member of the sanitary commission surprised no one. He likes to tell of disgusting conditions he has seen in other cities. While he was in Chicago at a medical convention he investigated a hotel charging the same price as the Pioneer House here in town, and he reported, all too graphically, how the ceiling was stained from leakage, how there was pencil writing on the walls, together with the husks of smashed roaches, and how he found a red hair embedded in the soap. Even the towel was rancid. Looking out the smoky window he saw wine bottles and decaying fruit in the gutter.

Visitors to this town often wonder how it is possible to exist without ballet, opera, and so forth, but it usually turns out that they themselves attend only once or twice each season, if at all. Then, too, if you are not accustomed to a certain entertainment you do not miss it. Russell, for example, grew up in a home devoid of music but cheerful and harmonious all the same. To his parents music was pointless, unless at Christmas time, when the phonograph would be wound up, the needle replaced, and the carols dusted off; consequently Mozart means nothing to him.

A Brooklyn police captain named Lehmbruck drove out here to spend his vacation but went back east after a week, saying it was too quiet to sleep. However he seemed to be interested in the sunset, remarking that he had never seen the sun go down anywhere except behind some buildings. And he had never eaten old ham—he studied the white specks very dubiously, and with some embarrassment asked if the ham was spoiled. The Chamber of Com-

merce later received a wistful little note from Captain
Lehmbruck, hinting that he might have another try at the
prairie next summer.

Christmas here is still made instead of bought, even if
we think no more of Christ than anyone else. And during
the summer months the sidewalks are overhung with white
or lavender spirea, and we can watch the rain approaching,
darkening the farmland. Life here is reasonable and tradi-
tion not discounted, as evidenced by the new public library which is a modified Parthenon of Tennessee marble.
There was a long and bitter argument about the inscription for its façade. One group wanted the so-called living
letter, while the majority sought reassurance in the Doric
past. At last we chiseled it with "Pvblic," "Covnty," "Strvc-
tvre," and so forth.

J. D. knew about all these things, but he must have
wanted more, and as he talked to us about his travels we
could read in his restless blue eyes that he was not through
searching. We thought he would come home when his father died, at least for a little while. Of course he was six
thousand miles away, but most men would have returned
from any distance. We did not know what he thought of
us, the friends who had been closest to him, and this was
altogether strange because our opinions about him were
no secret—the fact that Russell envied him and that Zobrowski thought his life was going to rot.

Russell, to be sure, envied everybody. For a time after
the marriage we believed Russell would collect himself,
whatever it was needed collecting, because he went around
looking very pleased with himself, although Eunice seemed
a bit confused. He began to go shooting in the hickory
woods again, firing his old .22 more to exult in its noise

than to kill a squirrel. Yet something within him had been destroyed. Whether it could have been an insufferable jealousy of J. D.—who was then in Finland—or love that was lost, or the hard core of another sickness unknown to anyone on earth, no one could say, but it was to be only a few years after J. D.'s visit that we would find Russell lying in the garage with his head almost torn off and a black .45 service automatic in his hand.

"Here is where Dante first met Beatrice," said J. D., adding with a smile that several locations in Florence claimed this distinction, even as half the apartments in Toledo insist El Greco painted there. And he had a picture of Cala Ratjada where he had lived with a Danish girl named Vivian. We had forgotten, if indeed we had ever realized it, that in other countries people are not required to be so furtive about their affairs. We learned that Cala Ratjada was a fishing village on the eastern end of Majorca. Majorca we had heard of because the vacation magazines were publicizing it.

"I understand there's a splendid cathedral in the capital," Zobrowski said. "Palma, isn't it?"

J. D. agreed rather vaguely. It was plain he did not care much for cathedrals, unless there was something queer about them as there was about the *Sagrada Familia*. He preferred to tell about the windmills on Majorca, and about his bus ride across the island with a crate of chickens on the seat beside him. We had not known there was a bus across the island; the travel magazines always advised tourists to hire a car with an English-speaking driver. So we listened, because there is a subtle yet basic difference between one who travels and one who does not.

He had lived with this Danish girl all of one summer in

a boarding house—a *pension* he called it—and every afternoon they walked through some scrubby little trees to a
white sandy beach and went swimming nude. They took
along a leather bag full of heavy amber wine and drank
this and did some fancy diving off the rocks. He said the
Mediterranean there at Cala Ratjada was more translucent
even than the harbor of Monte Carlo. When their wine
was finished and the sand had become cool and the shadows of the trees were touching the water they walked back
to the village. For a while they stopped on the embarca-
dero to watch the Balearic fishermen spreading their nets
to dry. Then J. D. and the Danish girl returned to the
pension for dinner. They ate such things as fried octopus,
or baby squid, or a huge seafood casserole called a *paella*.

"Where is she now?" Russell asked.

"Vivian?" said J. D. "Oh, I don't know. She sent me a
card from Frederikshavn a year or so ago. She'd been wanting to go to India, so maybe that's where she is now."

"Didn't she expect you to marry her?"

J. D. looked at Russell and then laughed out loud; it
was the first time he had laughed all evening.

"Neither of us wanted to get married," he said. "We had
a good summer. Why should we ruin it?"

This was a kind of reasoning we were aware of, via
novels more impressive for poundage than content; otherwise it bore no relation to us. What bound them together
was as elementary as a hyphen, and we suspected they
could meet each other years later without embarrassment.
They had loved without aim or sense, as young poets do.
We could imagine this, to be sure, but we could not imagine it actually happening. There were women in our
town, matrons now, with whom we had been intimate to

some degree a decade or so ago, but now when we met them, or were entertained in their homes, we were restrained by the memory of the delicate past. Each of us must carry, as it were, a balloon inked with names and dates.

So far as we knew, J. D. looked up only one of the women he used to know here in town. He called on Helen Louise Sawyer who used to win the local beauty contests. When we were young most of us were afraid of her, because there is something annihilating about too much beauty; only J. D. was not intimidated. Perhaps he could see then what we learned to see years later—that she was lonely, and that she did not want to be coveted for the perfection of her skin or for the truly magnificent explosion of her bosom. When Helen Louise and J. D. began going around together we were astonished and insulted because Russell, in those days, was much more handsome than J. D., and Dave Zobrowski was twice as smart. All the same she looked at no one else. Then he began leaving town on longer and longer expeditions. He would return wearing a southern California sport shirt, or with a stuffed grouper he had caught off Key West. Helen Louise eventually went into the real-estate business.

He telephoned her at the office and they went to dinner at the Wigwam, which is now the swank place to eat. It is decorated with buffalo skins and tomahawks and there are displays of flint arrowheads that have been picked up by farmers in neighboring counties. The only incongruities are the pink jade ashtrays that, by midnight, seem to have been planted with white, magenta-tipped stalks to remind the diners that a frontier has vanished. And well it has. The scouts are buried, the warriors mummified. Nothing but trophies remain: a coup stick hung by the Wigwam's flag-stone hearth, a pipe smoked by Satanta, a cavalry saber and a set of moldering blue gloves crossed on the mantel, a tan robe laced to the western wall, a dry Pawnee scalp behind the bar. The wind still sweeps east from the lofty Colorado plains, but carries with it now only the clank of machinery in the wheat fields. The Mandans have gone, like the minor chords of an Iowa death song, with Dull Knife and Little Wolf whose three hundred wretched squaws and starving men set out to fight their way a thousand miles to the fecund Powder River that had been their home.

There is a gratification to the feel of history behind the places one has known, and the Wigwam's historical display is extensive. In addition, the food is good. There is hot biscuit with clover honey, and the old ham so mistrusted by Captain Lehmbruck of Brooklyn. There are Missouri fried chicken, spare ribs, venison with mushrooms, cat-fish, beef you can cut with a fork, wild rice and duck buried under pineapple sauce, as well as various European dishes. That evening J. D. asked for a certain Madeira wine and apparently was a little taken aback to find that the Wigwam had it. Travelers, real travelers, come to think of their homes as provincial and are often surprised.

Helen Louise had metamorphosed, as even we could see, and we knew J. D. was in for a shock. Through the years she had acquired that faintly resentful expression that comes from being stared at, and she seemed to be trying to compensate for her beauty. Although there was nothing wrong with her eyes she wore glasses; she had cropped her beautiful golden hair to a Lesbian style; and somehow she did not even walk the way she used to. The pleasing un-dulations had mysteriously given way to a militant stride.

Her concern in life was over such items as acreage and location. At the business she was quite good; every real-estate man in town hated her, no doubt thinking she should have become a housewife instead of the demon that she was. But apparently she had lost her desire to marry, or sublimated it. At the lunch hour she could be seen in an expensive suit, speaking in low tones to another business-woman, and her conversation when overheard would be, ". . . referred the order to me . . . Mrs. Pabst's opinion . . . second mortgage . . . bought six apartments . . ."

We guessed that J. D.'s evening with Helen Louise might be an indication that he had grown tired of wandering around the earth, and that he wanted to come home for good. Helen Louise, if no longer as voluptuous as she had been at twenty or twenty-five, was still provocative, and if she married was it not possible she might come to look very much as she had looked ten years before? But J. D. had very little to say about his evening with her; and after he was gone Helen Louise never mentioned him.

"Did you know that in Cadiz," he said—because it was to him a fact worth noting, like the fact that in Lisbon he had lived on a certain plaza—"Did you know that in Cadiz you can buy a woman for three *pesetas?*" Whether or not he might have been referring to Helen Louise we did not know, nor did anyone ask.

"Once I talked with Manolete," he said, as though it were the first line of a poem.

"I've heard that name," Zobrowski answered. "He's a toreador, is he not?"

"I think 'toreador' was invented by Bizet," J. D. replied. "Manolete was a matador. But he's dead. It was in Linares that he was *cogido.* On the twenty-seventh of August in nineteen-forty-seven. At five in the afternoon, as the saying goes." And he continued, telling us that the real name of this bullfighter had been Manuel Rodriguez, and that after he was gored in Linares the ambulance which was taking him to a hospital started off in the wrong direction, and there was a feeling of bitterness in Spain when the news was broadcast that he was dead of his wounds.

"What you are trying to express," Zobrowski suggested, "is that this fellow was a national hero."

"Yes," said J. D.

"Like Babe Ruth."

"No," said J. D. instantly and with a vexed expression. He gestured helplessly and then shrugged. He went on to say that he happened to be in Heidelberg when death came for Manolete in the town of Linares. He looked around at us as if this circumstance were very strange. As he spoke he gestured excitedly and often skipped from one topic to another because there was so little time and he had so much to tell us. In a way he created a landscape of chiaroscuro, illuminating first one of his adventures and now another, but leaving his canvas mostly in shadow.

"One morning in Basle," he said, "it began to snow while I was having breakfast. Snow was falling on the Rhine." He was sitting by a window in a tea shop overlooking the river. He described the sunless, blue-gray atmosphere with large white flakes of snow piling up on the window ledge, and the dark swath of the river. Several waitresses in immaculate uniforms served his breakfast from a heavy silver tray. There was coffee in a silver pitcher, warm breads wrapped in thick linen napkins, and several kinds of jam and preserves; all the while the snow kept mounting on the ledge just outside the window, and the waitresses murmured in German. He returned to Basle on the same morning of the following year—all the way from Palermo—just to have his breakfast there.

Most of his ten years abroad had been spent on the borders of the Mediterranean, and he agreed with Zobrowski's comment that the countries in that area must be the dirtiest in Europe. He told about a servant girl in one of his *pensions* who always seemed to be on her knees scrubbing the floor, but who never bathed herself. She had such a pervasive odor that he could tell whenever she had recently been in a room.

He said that Pompeii was his biggest disappointment. He had expected to find the city practically buried under a cliff of lava. But there was no lava. Pompeii was like any city abandoned and overgrown with weeds. He had visited the Roman ruins of North Africa, but the names he mentioned did not mean anything to us. Carthage did, but if we had ever read about the others in school we had long since stored their names and dates back in the dusty bins alongside algebra and Beowulf. Capri was the only celebrated spot he visited that surpassed all pictures of it, and he liked Sorrento too, saying that he had returned to the mainland about sundown when the cliffs of Sorrento become red and porous like the cliffs of the Grand Canyon. And in a town called Amalfi he had been poisoned—he thought it was the eggs.

All this was delivered by a person we had known since childhood, yet it might as well have come from a foreign lecturer. J. D. was not trying to flaunt his adventures; he described them because we were his friends and he could not conceive of the fact that the ruins of Pompeii would mean less to us than gossip on the women's page. He wanted to tell us about the ballet in Cannes, where the audience was so quiet that he had heard the squeak of the dancer's slippers. But none of us had ever been to a ballet, or especially wanted to go. There was to us something faintly absurd about men and women in tights. When Zobrowski suggested as much, J. D. looked at him curiously and seemed to be struggling to remember what it was like to live in our town.

A number of things he said did not agree with our concept. According to him the Swedish girls are not in the least as they appear on calendars, which invariably depict them driving some cows down a pea-green mountainside. J. D. said the Swedes were long and gaunt with cadaverous features and gloomy dispositions, and their suicide rate was among the highest on earth.

Snails, he said, though no one had inquired, have very little taste. You eat them with a tiny two-pronged fork and some tongs that resemble a surgeon's forceps. The garlic-butter sauce is excellent, good enough to drink, but snail meat tasted to him rubbery like squid.

About the taxi drivers of Paris: they were incredibly avaricious. If you were not careful they would give you a gilded two-franc piece instead of a genuine fifty-franc piece for change, and if you caught them at it they became furious. But he did say that the French were the most urbane people to be found.

He had traveled as far east as Teheran and as far north as Trondheim. He had been to Lithuania and to Poland, and to Egypt and to the edge of the Sahara, and from his gestures as well as the animation of his voice we could tell he was not through yet. While he was telling us about his plans as we sat comfortably in the cocktail lounge of the

Pioneer House, a bellboy came in and respectfully said to Dave, "Dr. Zobrowski, the hospital is calling."

Without a word Zobrowski stood up and followed the boy. A few minutes later he returned wearing his overcoat and carrying his gray Homburg. "I'm sorry, but it's an emergency," he said to us all, and then to J. D., "Since you are not to be in town much longer I suppose this is good-by."

J. D. uncrossed his long legs and casually stood up.

"No doubt you lead an entertaining life," Zobrowski observed, not bothering to conceal his disapproval. "But a man cannot wander the face of the earth forever."

"That's what everybody tells me," J. D. answered with a grin. "It doesn't bother me much any more."

Zobrowski pulled on his yellow pigskin gloves and with a severe expression he began to settle the fingers as carefully as though he had put on surgical gloves. "In my opinion," he said suddenly, and lifted his eyes, "you are a damn fool."

They stared at each other for perhaps a minute, not with hostility, nor exactly with surprise, but as though they had never quite seen each other until that instant. Yet these were the two men who, about thirty years previously, had chipped in equal shares to buy a dog, a squat little beast with peculiar teeth that made it look like a beaver.

"From birth we carry the final straw," said Zobrowski at last.

J. D. only smiled.

Zobrowski's normally hard features contracted until he looked cruel, and he inclined his head, saying by this gesture, "As you wish." He had always known how to use silence with devastating force, yet J. D. was undismayed and did nothing but shrug like a Frenchman.

Zobrowski turned to Russell. "I had lunch with my broker the other day. He has some information on that Hudson's Bay mining stock of yours that makes me feel we should have a talk. Stop by my office tomorrow morning at eight-thirty. I have had my receptionist cancel an appointment because of this matter."

Russell's mouth slowly began to drop open as he gazed at Zobrowski. He never made reasonable investments and several times had been saved from worse ones only because he confided his financial plans, along with everything else, to anybody who would listen. Then, too, the making of money necessitates a callousness he had never possessed.

"That stock's all right," he said weakly. "I'm positive it's all right. Really it is, Dave. You should have bought some."

"Yes," Zobrowski said, looking down on him with disgust. And turning to J. D. he said, "Let us hear from you. Good-by." Then he went striding across the lounge.

"Oh, God!" mumbled Russell, taking another drink. He was ready to weep from humiliation and from anxiety over the investment. In the past few years he had become quite bald and flabby, and had taken to wearing suspenders because a belt disturbed his intestines. He rubbed his jowls and looked around with a vague, desperate air.

"Whatever happened to little Willie Grant?" J. D. asked, though Grant had never meant a thing to him.

"He's—he's in Denver," Russell said, gasping for breath.

"What about Martha Mathews?"

This was the girl who rejected Russell, but J. D. was

abroad when it happened and may never have heard. He
looked astonished when Russell groaned. Economically
speaking, she was a great deal better off than if she had
married Russell. She had accepted a housing contractor
with more ambition than conscience, and now spent
most of her time playing cards on the terrace of the country club.

J. D. had been in love, moderately, in the abstract, with
a long-legged sloe-eyed girl named Minnette whose voice
should have been poured into a glass and drunk. Her
mother owned a bakery. We usually saw Minnette's mother
when we came trotting home from school at the noon
hour; she would be standing at the door with arms rolled
in her apron while she talked to the delivery man, or, in
winter time, we would often see her as she bent over,
pendulous, tranquil, somehow everlasting, to place chocolate éclairs in the bakery window while sleet bounced in-
dignantly off the steaming glass. At such moments she
looked the way we always wanted our own harried moth-
ers to look. If the truth were known it might be that we
found her more stimulating than her daughter, although
this may have been because we were famished when we
passed the bakery. In any event he inquired about Minnette, so we told him her eyes still had that look, and that
she was married to the mortician, an extremely tall man
named Knopf who liked to underline trenchant phrases in
the little books on Success that you buy for a quarter.

Answering these somehow anachronistic questions
stirred us the way an old snapshot will do when you come
upon it while hunting for something else. Later on Russell
was to say that when J. D. mentioned the yellow brick
building where the four of us began our schooling he re-

membered for the first time in possibly a decade how we used to sit around a midget table and wield those short, blunt, red-handled scissors. We had a paste pot and sheets of colored paper, and when our labors were done the kindergarten windows displayed pumpkins, Christmas trees, owls, eggs, rabbits, or whatever was appropriate to the season. J. D. could always draw better than anyone else. When visiting night for parents came around it would be his work they admired. David Zobrowski, of course, was the scholar; we were proud to be Dave's best friends. Russell managed to remain undistinguished in any way until time for the singing class. Here no one could match him. Not that anyone wanted to. He sang worse than anyone who ever attended our school. It was as if his voice operated by a pulley, and its tenor was remotely canine. The class consisted of bluebirds and robins, with the exception of Russ who was placed at a separate desk and given no designation at all. Usually he gazed out the window at the interminable fields, but when it came to him that he, too, could sing, and his jaw began to work and his throat to contract, he would be warned into silence by the waving baton. It hurt his feelings very much.

Going to and from the business district ordinarily meant passing this musty little building, which had long since been converted into headquarters for the Boy Scout troop, and which now related to us no more than the Wizard of Oz, but until J. D. spoke of it we had not realized that the swings and the slide were gone, and crab grass was growing between the bricks of the front walk.

When we were in high school J. D. occasionally returned to wander through the corridors of the elementary school. The rest of us had been glad enough to move on and we considered his visits a bit queer, but otherwise never paused to think about them.

These were the streets where we had lived, these the houses, during a period of time when today could not influence tomorrow, and we possessed the confidence to argue about things we did not understand. Though, of course, we still did that. On winter nights we dropped away to sleep while watching the snow come drifting by the street light, and in summer we could see the moths outside the screens fluttering desperately, as though to tell us something. Our childhood came and went before we were ready to grasp it. Things were different now. The winged seeds that gyrate down from the trees now mean nothing else but that we must sweep them from the automobile hood because stains on the finish lower the trade-in value. Now, in short, it was impractical to live as we used to live with the abandon of a mule rolling in the dust.

In those days our incipient manhood had seemed a unique power, and our single worry that some girl might become pregnant. We danced with our eyes closed and our noses thrust into the gardenias all the girls wore in their hair, meanwhile estimating our chances. And, upon discovering literature, thanks to the solemn pedantry of a sophomore English teacher, we affected bow ties and cigarette holders and were able to quote contemporary poets with a faintly cynical tone.

On a postcard of a Rotterdam chocolate factory, sent to Russell but addressed to us all, J. D. scribbled, "I see nothing but the noon dust a-blowing and the green grass a-growing." If not contemporary it was at least familiar, and caused Zobrowski to remark, with a certain unconscious measure, "As fond as I am of him I sometimes lose patience. In a furrow he has found a feather of Pegasus and what should have been a blessing has become a curse."

Now J. D. was inquiring after one or two we had forgotten, or who had moved away, leaving no more trace than a cloud, and about a piano teacher who had died one sultry August afternoon on the streetcar. Yet his interest was superficial. He was being polite. He could not really care or he would not have gone away for ten years. He wondered whatever became of the bearded old man who used to stand on a street corner with a stack of Bibles and a placard promising a free copy of the New Testament to any Jew who would renounce the faith. We did not know what happened to the old man; somehow he had just vanished. Quite a few things were vanishing.

J. D. cared very little for the men who had once been our fraternity brothers, which was odd because in our hearts we still believed that those days and those men had been so extraordinary that people were still talking about them. Yet we could recall that he took no pride in being associated with them. The militant friendship of fraternity life made him surly. He refused to shake hands as often as he was expected to. We had been warned that, as pledges, we would be thrown into the river some night. This was part of learning to become a finer man. When the brothers came for us about three o'clock one morning, snatching away our blankets and singing the good fellowship song, we put up the traditional fight—all of us except J. D. He refused to struggle. He slumped in the arms of his captors as limp as an empty sack. This puzzled and annoyed the brothers, who held him aloft by his ankles and who bounced his head on the floor. He would not even open his eyes. They jabbed him stiffly in the ribs, they twisted his arms behind his back, they kicked him in the pants, they called him names, and finally, very angry, they dragged him to the river and flung him in. But even when he went sailing over the bullrushes he was silent as a corpse. Strangely, he did not hit the water with a loud splash. Years later he told us that he twisted at the last moment and dove through the river scum, instead of landing flat on his back as Russell did. They vanished together, as roommates should, but Russell was again audible in a few seconds—thrashing back to shore, where the brothers helped him out and gave him a towel and a bathrobe and a drink of brandy.

J. D., however, did not reappear. Even before Russell had reached the shore we were beginning to worry about J. D. There was no moon that night and the river had an evil look. We stood in a row at the edge of the water. We heard the bullfrogs, and the dark bubbling and plopping of whatever calls the river home, but nothing more. And all at once the structure of the fraternity collapsed. The last vestige of unity disappeared. We were guilty individuals. Some people began lighting matches and peering into the river, while others called his name. But there was no answer, except in the form of rotten, half-submerged driftwood floating by, revolving in the sluggish current, and, beyond the confused whispering, the brief, crying shadows of night birds dipping in wild alarm over the slimy rushes.

When we saw him again we asked what happened, but several years passed before he told anyone. Then he said —and only then was his revenge complete—"Oh, I just swam under water as far as I could. After that I let the river carry me out of sight." He swam ashore a mile or two downstream, and by a back road he returned to the fraternity house. Nobody was there; everybody was at the river searching for his body. The fraternity was almost ruined because of J. D.

Now he had climbed the Matterhorn, and we were not surprised. He knew what it was like in Venice, or in Copenhagen, and as we reflected on his past we came to understand that his future was inevitable. We knew he would leave us again, perhaps forever.

Russell, tamping out a cheap cigar, said boldly, "Eunice and I have been thinking about a trip to the Bahamas next year, or year after." He considered the nicotine on his fingertips, and after a pause, because his boast was empty, and because he knew that we knew how empty it was, he added, "Though it depends." He began picking helplessly at his fingertips. He would never go anywhere.

"You'll like the Bahamas," J. D. said.

"We consider other places," Russell said unexpectedly, and there were tears in his eyes.

J. D. was watching him with a blank, pitiless gaze.

"I think I'll go to Byzantium," Russell said.

"That doesn't exist any more."

Russell took a deep breath to hush the panic that was on him, and at last he said, "Well, gentlemen, I guess I'd better get some shut-eye if I'm going to talk business with Dave in the morning."

"It's late," J. D. agreed.

Then we asked when he would be coming home for good, although it was a foolish question, and J. D. laughed at it. Later, in talking about him, we would recall his reason for not wanting to live here. He had explained that the difference between our town and these other places he had been was that when you go walking down a boule-

vard in some strange land and you see a tree burgeoning
you understand that this is beautiful, and there comes
with the knowledge a moment of indescribable poignance
in the realization that as this tree must die, so will you die.
But when, in the home you have always known, you find
a tree in bud you think only that spring has come again.
Here he stopped. It did not make much sense to us, but for
him it had meaning of some kind.

So we asked when he would be coming back for another
visit. He said he didn't know. We asked what was next. He
replied that as soon as he could scrape together a few more
dollars he thought he might like to see the Orient.

"They say that in Malaya . . ." he began, with glowing
eyes. But we did not listen closely. He was not speaking to
us anyway, only to himself, to the matrix which had
spawned him and to the private god who guided him. His
voice reached us faintly, as if from beyond the walls of
Ávila.

I Came from Yonder Mountain

Beyond the upcountry of the Carolinas, farther back in the hills where the clay looks blue and the wild carrot and yellow lily cover the scars of crumbled sawmills, where thunder has the high rattling sound of pebbles in a wood bucket, there the ridges are hung with scented air in the heart of the afternoon and there if you wander into a hollow sometimes you'll catch a far-off smell of sweet bay or see the pendant bells of a honeycup swinging in the wind. There the red spruce and the paintbrush grow, bordering trails that spiral down the mountains, and if the long clouds resembling cliffs of slate appear in the west then there will fall drops of rain big around as acorns.

It was on such a day that a girl wound down the trail to a town called Keating, which was a town shaped like an oak leaf with a railroad track for a stem. The girl's name was Laurel Wyatt and she carried under one arm, wrapped in a crazy-patch quilt, her baby which did not very often move. She did not look at the baby, but once in a while she spoke to it, as though it were a grown person.

" 'Tis a piece," she said in that fashion, looking mildly ahead.

A wind shook the sides of her black sweater and twisted

those strings of her hair not bound by the ribbon behind her neck. Cinnamon squirrels sailed along the tree limbs considering her through quick eyes, while in the woods flickers called and bloodheads knocked suddenly and then were answered by thunder sounding far in the west. The sun overhead filtered through the southern pines like streamers of yellow gauze; insects with wings thin as spotted tissue flickered in the light.

A raindrop thumped the crazy-patch quilt. Another pounded into the trail, thereby causing a dust umbrella to open beside the girl's foot.

"Powerful day," she said to the baby.

Across log bridges where excited water popped and slipped on rocks, past raccoons who stopped their dark and slender hands to watch her, softly on a pad of brown pine needles Laurel moved down toward the town of Keating. The streams as she passed over them were white and green, and moss tails which were stuck to the rocks swayed in the current. Once one broke free and wiggled quickly downstream as though it were alive. Once as she crossed a log bridge there fell from its underside a chain of fat bugs which floated gravely away. Water spiders skated in pools behind rocks; bits of pine branch also revolved and sometimes a stiff cone.

She came to a stream where on the far side a baby hog bear sliced the water again and again and each time looked in wonder at its empty paw. Laurel stood by a hollow stump and at last the bear sat up and, seeing her, trundled away into the woods like a small barrel.

Thunder rattled as she moved over a bald. Rocks in her path were speckled with mica which threw back the light of the sun, and by them copper thorns overhanging the trail grabbed at her ankles but each one slid over her stiff skin. In the woods again, she set her baby on the ground in order to fasten the little buttons of her sweater. Then on she went, and down.

When she came to the clearing of a cabin she stopped by the cistern there and with a porcelain dipper took water from the bucket. Brown smoke rose a few feet above the cabin and then spread out like a toadstool. A man in brown coveralls sat in the cabin doorway and raised one hand to her but she did not see him. She put the dipper back in the bucket and walked past the clearing and on down the trail.

A flarehawk coasted over with tail spread and beak hooked bitterly: in the branches and on the ground nothing moved. Wandering clouds crackled, shot quick forks at one another which sometimes bent down to test the strength of the red spruce trees, and once as Laurel Wyatt crossed a charred tract there floated silently from one cloud a ball of green fire.

"This heart of Judas," she said. And scarce looked at it though the fire followed her to the trees.

Beyond another bald a shower caught her, and her black sweater sagged with water. On she walked, across ridges where the false loblolly grew and down through the following hollows by a preacher's message painted on a flat stone, on until at last she came to the doorstoops of Keating whereon lay bent rakes and barrel hoops and dozing hounds with mange. Through the town she went to the railroad platform and there she laid the baby beside her on a bench, crossed her legs, and sat looking straight ahead.

On the platform stood a man with a pink face and eyebrows like scrolls of birchbark; behind him sat a woman who wore a dress with three-cornered buttons. The man ducked his head and squinted at Laurel.

"Oh, stop clowning," the woman said.

He strode the platform with his lips pressed together.

"Must you eternally pace?" she asked.

"There it is. It can't get up the hill."

"Must you say something funny every minute?"

Then nobody spoke for a long time until down the line the train gave a hoot and chuggled up the tracks with feathers of steam spurting out from the engine wheels. The number on its hood was 7. The wheels squeaked as the train prepared to stop. When this had been done all that moved was the iron bell atop the cab which swung back and forth emptying itself drunkenly over the platform. Then a coach door clanked and the conductor stepped down, a tiny man with hook-and-lace shoes and a nose like an orange rind.

Quickly the man picked up two suitcases and the woman pushed a parcel, a gourd, and a canvas jacket under his arm.

"Sweetheart, you're tired?" he asked. She climbed the steps and he followed, staring at the back of her head. "You're tired?" he asked, disappearing into the coach.

The conductor smelled of stout tobacco. He walked up and down the gray boards dragging one foot and rubbing his arms while the iron bell on the cab clanged and rolled north, clanged and rolled south.

"What you going to wear for a wedding coat?" caroled the conductor in a sharp voice. He walked to the end of the platform where he spit onto the tracks and stood looking behind the train at the western mountains. Sparks and ashes drifted above him. He turned around and walked back along the railroad platform. "Old chin whiskers of a billy goat," he sang. He stood at the other end of the platform for several minutes, came back, and climbed aboard the train.

Laurel Wyatt sat with one hand resting on her crossed thighs. The bottom of the pale dress was above her knees.

The conductor banged half of the door, and Laurel's eyes focused. She walked to the closed train door where she said, "I am locally."

Came the voice of the conductor: "Too late."

"I have come to train travel," she said.

The conductor slowly opened the door. Laurel Wyatt went into a coach and sat down, putting the baby beside her. She sat as on the bench with one hand resting on her thigh and the other on the seat.

The couplings rattled, clanked, the coach knocked backward then forward and began to move.

The toes of the baby curled but it made no sound. About its wrist was tied a string with seven knots.

"For I'm a-going—I'm a-going away—" In came the conductor, the black leather of his hook-and-lace shoes squirking. "Whereabouts you folks headed?"

"Out of these queer hills," said the man. "That girl's cracked. I can't understand her. She gives me the creeps."

"Everything gives you the creeps."

"You're tired, sweetheart? You're not feeling good again?"

"They're like that. Yes, sir. They are. I seen them time and again. Time and again do it. They think the train waits specially for them. But it don't. No, sir!" The conductor went along the aisle patting the top of each seat. "For to stay—a little while—"

He stopped beside Laurel. "Them folks inform me you been sitting there nearabouts an hour waiting on this train. You deef? What's the matter with you? We set by that station there eight minutes, you didn't get on. I expect largely you be a deef one. Hey? This train come up the hills, set by eight minutes, you don't fleck a muscle. Only got a number of minutes in Keating. They's a storm fixing to swamp us. People think trains set by all day long waiting for them specially, they don't, don't do nothing specially. Not for nobody. I expect you know that. Hey? Don't you? Don't that appeal to you? Eight minutes is all. You be deef. Ain't you? What's the matter with you?"

"I presume largely I forgot it," Laurel said, but she did not look at the conductor.

"You do! You do! Ahahah!" The conductor pinched the end of his nose in rage. "Give me your money. Whereabouts you headed? Tipton? You mountain people always go to Tipton. That's where you be headed. Tipton'll cost you exactly a dollar and ten cents."

Laurel cautiously folded her hands.

"Whereabouts you headed? Tipton?"

But she did not answer.

"You be headed for Tipton."

"I came from yonder mountain."

The conductor bent his knees and sank down a little to peer out the window. "Deef or no deef, give me the money for Tipton."

"I have that money," Laurel said, reaching into the pocket of her sweater. "And here. 'Tis the money for a train travel to Tipton town." She added, "I have quite a considerable of this money." And then she sucked in her lips and looked at the floor of the coach.

The conductor put the money in his coat pocket and moved along dragging one foot. "But I'm a-coming back —if I go ten thousand mile—if I go ten thousand mile."

Laurel rested her hands in her lap and watched the telephone poles go by. She did not move, but sat mile after mile in that same fashion while the train clicked along with the rhythm of a galloping horse, and all that showed she was not a stone girl was a softness to her cheeks when the train screeched around a curve and the late afternoon sun touched the pale hairs of her face.

As the train sank and moved south the clay cutbacks became stippled with gravel and changed in color; they were almost white, then pink, and when the train clacketed over a bare patch the clay had broken through the topsoil in a scarlet web. The train rolled between wooden sheds on which were nailed crusty tin medicine signs, and crossed a street where bells were ringing and a man swung a lantern. Then the train was dark, for clay banks rose beside the windows, and when these banks dropped to let in the sun there was no town.

Laurel Wyatt stood up. The train swayed and she fell into the seat. She stood again and held on to the baggage rack above the seats. With her hands high above her head she looked around the coach.

"Tipton town?" she asked in a voice very low.

Her body swayed with the motion of the train and as she hung almost by her hands the pale printed dress pulled above her knees. Her legs were short and solid. Below her knees the skin was tan and stiff, but higher it was white and soft.

"Oh, my Lord!" she said.

As the train went around a curve her hip bumped the window and then she swung out into the coach. She looked over the seat toward the corridor at the rear where the conductor had disappeared. She was standing tiptoe, her fingers hooking through the wire mesh of the rack. She clung there as the tracks curved twice more.

Then, "Smoke Hill 'twas," she said, unhooked her fingers from the mesh and dropped into the seat.

It was as she sat down that rain came tapping softly on her window, and the sky braided with clouds. The fields which had lain flat by the wheels humped into ridges and were now the sides of a trough wherein the ashes of the train collected, and the coaches tipped downward with squealing wheels while orange sparks flicked by. Through the trough with windows rattling, couplings banging, went the train. Then onto flat fields it rushed, and there was Tipton.

The iron bell rang and turned east and rang and turned west.

"What'll the wedding supper be?" the conductor sang. Laurel's sweater caught on the door handle and he pulled it free for her to step down, singing, "Dogwood soup and catnip tea."

Beyond the platform in the distance rose the eagle's beak of the mountain. Turning until it overhung her left shoulder, Laurel Wyatt entered the city of Tipton, cheeks sucked in, dropping each foot as though into a deep hole. A hedge grew before her; she pushed through it while people watched, then on through flowers bound to stakes. Her feet dragged over a slab of writing. On she went, looking to neither side, by a wrought-iron bench, under the broken stone sword of a horseman riding north.

Beyond painted lines she entered a street and she paused, looked over her shoulder again for the eagle's beak. Then on till a building was in her path. She stopped, struck once at the door, and stood waiting.

There came through the shutters above a woman's voice. "What do you want? His office is closed."

Laurel Wyatt stood by the door.

"Come back tomorrow."

As the day darkened the voice called out again, "I told you to go. I said tomorrow."

Much later: "Good Lord, you still there? Oh, I'll tell him."

Later still, by the landing window a light was carried; a lamp turned on. In the doorway the doctor buttoned his vest. "Well, girl?"

He took off his glasses, twirled them slowly by the white ear pieces, looked at the baby. "You know that child is dead. You know that."

To the door came a nurse with a soft doughy face. She stood beside the doctor, looking at the baby. "I should think it is dead."

"Blister plasters," muttered the doctor. "If it wasn't dead before, you'd have murdered it with those plasters. You know that, don't you?"

"I doubt if she does," said the nurse.

"Somebody ought to go back in those hills and teach you people. Everybody knows I'm too busy, but somebody ought to."

"I told her. I said, 'Come back tomorrow.' "

Though Laurel spoke the words could scarcely be heard. " 'Tis dead."

They watched her for a moment.

"Why didn't your husband come along with you, girl?"

"He's probably drunk," said the nurse.

"Where are you from?"

"She doesn't even know."

"You've come a long way down out of those hills, girl. A long way. You got enough money to get back? You do, don't you?"

"She hasn't got any money. She hasn't got anything."

"You take that child back. You give it a fine burial."

"She doesn't even hear you."

"Nobody ever hears what I say. Nobody ever does. All right, girl. Give it to me. I'll see it's done."

"She'd probably drop it in a ditch."

Laurel stood looking beyond their shoulders and the lamp in the hallway darkened the sockets of her cheeks, caught a glisten in her eyes. A raindrop came down her temple and the cheekbone, rested on her jaw. Slowly, slanting into the doorway where Laurel Wyatt stood, the heavy rain began to fall. Water streamed down her arms and curved through her empty palms, dripped from her fingertips. The pale dress, wet, wrapped slowly around her legs.

Through the rain she moved, past the sloshing window ledges of shuttered buildings, through boundaries of sticks and paint, beyond the stoppered mouths of settling cannon, beyond awnings and wires whereon the bulbs of Tipton flickered, upon the black and silent cinders until they had sunk in clay, and on, with the rhythm of a slow pulse beat, into the edge of a forest where at last among trunks of spruce the sound of her passage was lost in the rain.

The Color of the World

If you'd ask Mrs. Passen about Shannon McCambridge, she'd likely fold her veiny hands together and say, "The Lord will destroy him." If you'd asked her about the Widow Gorman, she might turn away without even answering. Mrs. Passen is sort· of the link between God and Cow Lake.

Cow Lake was built in 1827 in the middle of the prairie. Now it's in the middle of the Kansas wheat fields, but outside of that nothing much has changed. Only two things break up the squares of wheat. One is the creek bed that cuts behind the grave-digger's shack, and sometimes has water in it during March. The other is a bunch of black pins that stick up off to the south. Those are oil derricks, but the oil men quit a long time ago. The derricks are rusting. Life comes pretty hard in southern Kansas. Maybe once a month some of the folks go over to Wichita.

Dust covers almost everything. If a car goes by, dust winds up from the concrete and settles on the silent dogs that lie against the curbs. If one of the dogs walks somewhere its trail is marked for several minutes by a row of dust mushrooms.

There's no saliva on the lips of the women who go to Mrs. Passen's every Wednesday to gain strength from the Gospel, and there's no sweat on the Widow Gorman when she comes into town, except under her arms. There's no whisky on the counter in back of Dummy's pool hall, but the folks who like to drink make Dummy keep the counter there. They like to look at it. The farmers never talk about it, but when they're in town they go over to Dummy's to look at it. They feel of its slick brown top and suck at their teeth for a while.

A little bit after the sun comes up the side doors of the houses open and old women come out. They have celluloid fans that advertise a hardware store. They sit on the porches until sundown, waving the fans. Most of them sit in swings that have chains screwed into the roofs. When they get up at noon or when they pull at their cotton stockings the chains squeak.

All day the sun is blue-white. It crumbles the thin dirt roads into a powder that sticks to everything. On the highway the tar strips turn to jelly, and blue flies cover the little animals killed by touring cars.

Nobody ever looks for clouds.

The Widow Gorman lives out beyond the edge of town. When it begins to cool off around five o'clock she'll sometimes drive in for things like a packet of raspberry coloring or a movie magazine. The young men who sit on the steps of the houses late in the afternoon don't say anything when she goes by. After she's gone they begin to pick at little clots of mud, or they sit on their fingers, or look at the cement. They never look at each other. The old men don't say anything. The women who sit on the porches don't say anything. The chains never squeak when the Widow goes by.

Finally the sun goes down and the people begin to take off their clothes.

Mrs. Passen is five feet eleven inches tall and her ankles are almost as big around as her neck. She owns the boarding house. The shades are always pulled. Folks who've lived longest in town say they don't know what would happen to religion if Mrs. Passen should ever go to her Reward, but it doesn't seem like she ever will.

She sings at all the men's funerals. She sings at weddings, too, but sometimes she'll drive clear to Parallel if there's a big funeral for a man scheduled. It's close to fifty miles to Parallel, but Mrs. Passen takes time to go over and sing hymns. She never takes any money for her singing, although it's sort of understood that whenever she sings at a man's funeral his widow gives her a photograph of him. She keeps them in a black tin box in the cellar. But she says they give her a deeper Meaning, so now and again she brings them up and spreads them across the dining-room table.

Mr. Passen disappeared just three weeks after their daughter was born. He disappeared in Oklahoma City, where he used to drive to sell more insurance. Some officers came up on the train from Oklahoma and told Mrs. Passen they'd found a body, only they weren't satisfied it was the body of Mr. Passen. They stayed several days, asking if he'd ever looked at the ladies more than was right and wanting to know if he'd gotten mail from out of town. But finally they looked at each other and went back to Oklahoma.

After they'd gone Mrs. Passen told how she'd had a Visitation. The Savior had come and said because her little girl had been born with a crooked foot she should be named Faith, and the Savior had begged Mrs. Passen to pray for the child.

All through her early grades in school Faith was at the top of her class, and even as far as fifth grade she was pretty well along, but then she began to get shy. So when company came to the boarding house Mrs. Passen liked her to skip rope for them instead of reciting "Hiawatha" or "The Children's Hour" as most of the other little girls did. She said that was the best thing for her shyness. The guests always clapped, even though Faith sometimes got tangled up in the piece of clothesline she used for rope.

When her tenth birthday came around she asked her mother for a box of paints and a brush, but Mrs. Passen said the Lord had painted the world. She said now that she was ten it was time to learn about the Lord, and she said Faith should be proud because the Savior had given her one of his crucified legs.

When she was twelve Faith's hair began to grow silky, and took on more the color of wheat just before it was cut, and her breasts swelled so the older boys watched her, and her lips turned more red and she began to laugh and sing a little sometimes, and she learned to carve kittens out of soap. But life doesn't come easy in southern Kansas. Mrs. Passen had to cook the kittens into lumps so the soap could be used.

That summer Faith met the Widow Gorman. She was standing outside R. L. Boehm's bakery when the Widow came out with a sack of cakes, and they looked at each other and both of them smiled, and the Widow said if she'd carry the cakes to the car she could have one. When Faith began to walk the Widow clapped her hand to her mouth. She didn't look at Faith's foot, but she took the cakes and said she had some shopping to do, and she hurried into the lobby of the movie house. Faith started to follow her. Then she quit. She put her arms around the post of a streetlight on the curb and hugged the iron.

The Widow came back out. She asked Faith who she was, and after Faith had told her the Widow didn't say anything for almost a minute. Then she said, "Good God!" She took Faith into the ice-cream parlor where she bought her a root-beer soda and gave her a dollar, and kissed her on the forehead.

Faith bought a box of paints in Keeven's dime store. She took the box to the elm trees in back of Leroy Bates' house. Bates' is on a little rise and there under the elms she could see almost to Wichita. She looked out across the fields until dinner time, and she hid the paint box in a stump before she went home.

That night Mrs. Passen asked for the dollar, and when she didn't have it Mrs. Passen took her out next to the garbage cans and together they knelt, asking forgiveness of the Lord. While they were kneeling Mrs. Passen said the Widow Gorman would be struck by the hand of the Almighty because her soul was more diseased than garbage.

Faith began to spend all her afternoons in back of Bates' under the elm trees. She'd sit there painting big golden pictures of the wheat fields and orange and purple sunsets.

It almost never rains in Cow Lake during the summer, so she rolled up her paintings and wrapped them around the handle of the black umbrella in the closet. She left the boarding house early every morning so she could be out in the fields when the sun rose. She told her mother it was like church on Christmas Eve. Mrs. Passen thought for a while, but didn't say anything.

When she was almost fourteen, one of the boys asked Mrs. Passen if he could take Faith to his high-school party in the gym at Wichita. But Mrs. Passen said no because when Faith finished high school she was going to study at the Eternal Heart, and it wouldn't be right. She told Faith she was sorry, and she invited the boy to stay a while, but he blinked a few times through his heavy glasses and then said he had to go home. Faith told him good-by at the front door; she thanked him for asking. Then she took the Bible she had gotten for her birthday and went out to the twin elm trees, but she didn't read the passages her mother had told her to memorize; she only sat there until way after sundown, her eyes round and empty like she was blind.

Oron Duchein brought her a box of peanut brittle on her fifteenth birthday, but Mrs. Passen gave it to the gravedigger after Oron went home because it had gone sour in the heat. She patted Faith on the head and told her she was sending clear to Kansas City for an eight-dollar shoe for her foot.

It was three days after that when Mrs. Passen sprang open the umbrella to see if it needed mending, and the pictures of the sunsets unrolled and dropped to the floor.

She called Faith home from school. Then she looked at the pictures for a long time while Faith sat cross-legged at her feet. Faith's eyes were soft and big while she waited, and her lips quivered. She sat on the floor waiting to throw her arms around her mother's neck and cry and kiss her, and cry some more—to cry in her mother's arms until the pain was all gone, but Mrs. Passen got out her shears and cut each of the pictures into eight oblong pieces that would fit into the black box with the photographs of men. She said again that the Lord had painted the world.

Mrs. Passen had more than her share of troubles. Everybody in Cow Lake had troubles. Some of them had sickness every year during the rainy season, others would lose their crops, and some would always be living on a mortgage. But everybody said Mrs. Passen had the most troubles, especially after Faith drowned.

It was at night. Shannon McCambridge found her next morning on his way home from the Widow Gorman's. Faith had drowned in the wading pool. Her hair was still tawny and wonderfully soft, like the wheat, and Shannon McCambridge said it floated under the surface of the pool like the wheat fields sometimes rippled and seemed to float under the wind. Her bad foot was all doubled up, he said, but the specially built shoe from Kansas City was safe on the bank.

Mrs. Passen had a portrait of Faith painted from an old photograph and she hung it in the parlor, and over the portrait she hung a framed piece of crepe that had her favorite passage woven into it: "O Lord, how excellent is thy name in all the earth!"

The Widow Gorman sent a note asking if she could buy

a little rose garden for the church, but Mrs. Passen burned the note and flushed the ashes down the toilet. She got into her black dress again, the same dress she had put on when her husband went to his Reward. She ordered a purple candle from a funeral house in Denver, and she hung it under the portrait so some light would always shine on Faith.

Everybody in town came to comfort Mrs. Passen and they all told her she was the most courageous woman they had ever known. Generally when they told her Mrs. Passen would fold her veiny hands together and murmur, "The good Lord giveth and the good Lord taketh away."

++

The Trellis

Inspector Polajenko stood in the middle of the street with his gloved hands cupped around his mouth as if he were shouting through the rain; actually he was only shielding his cigar. While he smoked he gazed at a purple stucco cottage which indicated by an absence of lace curtains that a man lived there alone, and according to a sign on the front gate the man was a silversmith named Tony Miula.

Though it was only a few minutes after dawn there were lights in almost every neighboring house and faces could be seen at upstairs windows. A cluster of motorcycles and a police sedan were parked before the yellow brick Colonial house next door to Tony Miula's cottage.

Inspector Polajenko splashed across the street, unhooked Miula's gate, and walked toward the front door with a bemused expression, like a philosopher who has stumbled on a great truth. The door opened before his fist had touched it and Polajenko, who was not a little man, looked up at Tony Miula.

Calmly the inspector said, "I've heard about you," wiped his shoes on the mat, and stepped inside the cottage.

"What have you heard?" asked Miula in a nasal tenor.

He had been cutting pictures out of a magazine and still carried the scissors.

Polajenko walked to a window where he could see the sleeping porch of the neighboring house. After a few seconds he walked to another window from which he could again see the sleeping porch and a part of the back yard where, in a corner, stood an arch of white latticework interlaced with rose bushes. Elegant red and yellow blossoms burst everywhere through this trellis, some of them touching the legs and back of a wicker chair in which an obese, bald-headed man was sitting.

"Just your name," he said, and a friendly little smile came onto his face.

Tony looked relieved.

"How much do you pay for this bungalow?" Polajenko asked, moving to another window where he continued to stare at the bald-headed man, who was wearing a raincoat over some gaudy pajamas and who seemed very much at peace because his legs were crossed and one hand rested casually in his lap. On one knee hung a checkered golfing cap. His head was tilted back as though he sat in a dentist's chair, while the September rain streamed steadily down his face.

"The rent is five hundred dollars a year," replied Tony, following the inspector with glittering eyes, "but I think that's too much so I just pay four hundred and ninety-nine, and every year the landlord gets furious."

"I keep forgetting the name of your neighbor," said Polajenko.

"I don't believe you," Tony said, snapping the scissors, but as the inspector did not comment he finally muttered, "Allan Ehe."

"Ah, yes," Polajenko said, looking from the trellis to the screened-in porch, "now I remember."

"Do you know what I did during the war?" Tony asked.

"I'm a little afraid to guess," Polajenko answered and continued twisting the left side of his mustache.

"Every day, all day, for more than three years I cleaned out the officers' latrines. Do you know why? Because I refused to fire a weapon even for practice."

"Well, Tony, it is a fine idea to object; however you must pay for the luxury."

"I cannot possibly fire a gun."

"Did I say you killed Allan Ehe?" Polajenko assumed a pained expression.

Tony Miula crossed his legs and sat down regal and serene as a yogi. Around him the carpet was littered with magazine pages and metal staples he had pried from the bindings in order to dismantle each publication completely.

"How do you make your living, my friend?" inquired the inspector, standing at a window with his back to Tony Miula.

"I'm a bachelor, as you know, with little living to make."

"How do you know I know?"

Tony ignored him.

"Let us suppose you had a wife, my friend, how would you pay for her?"

"I would work with my hands."

"Would you make those sandals you wear?"

"Yes, I would," said Tony after some thought. "Furthermore I might tool leather belts and engrave silver buckles. Possibly you noticed the sign in front?"

"Ah," the inspector said, snapping his fingers, "I remember now that I did." From his vest he took a new cigar and began carefully sliding it from the cellophane. "Have you known this neighbor very long?"

"Years and years. We were introduced when he was thirteen and I was nine. He immediately hit me in the eye."

"Have you been fighting ever since?"

"Yes, indeed. I always got the best of him."

Polajenko had crumpled the cellophane in his fist and now dropped it to the carpet.

"Pick that up," Tony ordered. "It's not the same as a clipping."

Polajenko hastily did as he was told, and while putting the cellophane in the pocket of his raincoat he asked, "Do you drink a great deal?"

"Whenever I cannot handle the weight of the world."

Polajenko was sympathetic. "How often is that?"

"Never."

"You don't seem very strong to me."

"You'd be surprised," said Tony, not looking up from his magazines.

"Where do you sleep?"

"I sleep on the lawn in summer."

"Will you tell me why?"

"To watch the cardinals which live in a bush nearby."

"Well, my metronomic man, where do you sleep in the winter time?"

"On a cot by the kitchen stove."

"You are a strange piece of goods," the inspector said. "I must get to know you better."

"You will," said Tony, prying out a staple with the tip of his scissors.

Polajenko began to wander around the room with his head bowed and hands behind his back. Tony glanced with annoyance at the drops of water his raincoat was shedding but said nothing. The only sounds in the bungalow were the snip of the scissors and a damp squeaking of the inspector's shoes as he circled the man on the floor.

"I've seen thousands of hands," Polajenko resumed. "Like a face, a hand has a few lines in the play. In you I discern a little of Baudelaire, and believe me, my friend, there is nothing farther from the soul of a decent American than Baudelaire."

"Inspector," said Tony after a pause, "would you like to know why the man is dead?"

"Why else would I be here?"

Tony dropped his scissors, crossed his arms on his chest and looked up at the inspector. "That's not worthy of you, sir. Neither of us is a fool."

Polajenko looked apologetic but said nothing.

"I cannot tell you all the reasons he is dead, but I can tell you more than anyone else, more than his wife, or more than his mother, of whom I am very fond and for whom I always create something nice at Christmas time. I can tell you what insults he never forgot and why, about Jeanne Williams and Jean Williams, or the treasure hunt by which I delayed his suicide. I am able to analyze his friends; I knew them infinitely better than he ever did or could. Friendships begin by accident but end on purpose. It is true that a foolish hostess may cry, 'Martin Gorst, this is George Boom. You two will be inseparable!' But if Gorst and Boom look at one another favorably it will come to pass in spite of their introduction and no one will know why. Though it may be true that providence can separate two men for life still they are friends and will remain so until the chemistry of their relationship has changed, which is not an accident. Sometimes the two who were bound in this way understand why they are no longer so, but sometimes they do not, knowing only that they will inconvenience themselves to avoid any sight or sound of the other. Then again, one may perceive and one not perceive—which is the way it generally was with myself and this unstable individual who is now being removed feet first from the back yard."

Inspector Polajenko, who had been looking out the window, instantly turned around but Tony was still seated on the floor.

"Tell me, my friend, just how do you know he is being carried away?"

"I hear them talking in the back yard," replied Tony. "There are three men. Two of them are subordinates."

Polajenko closed his eyes and cocked his head, but he could hear only the splash of water from the eaves and the tick of the watch deep in his vest.

"They've forgotten his cap," Tony added.

Immediately Polajenko looked out the window. The lieutenant was just stooping beside the trellis where Ehe's golfing cap lay upside down in the wet grass. Two motorcycle policemen walked across the back yard with the body on a stretcher.

"I must get to know you better," said Polajenko tightly.

"I told you you would," said Tony.

With a thoughtful expression Polajenko suggested, "I have a friend who would like to meet you."

"He has a good practice, I'm sure."

Polajenko looked dourly at the silversmith.

"When Allan was very young he did a cruel thing," Tony said, and disgust ran lightly across his face.

"Who has not? The trick is to feign ignorance of it."

"These two girls named Williams were not related but they lived on the same street and one was very popular. Allan lacked the courage to approach her so one night he opened the telephone book, found a Williams on the proper street, and made his call. He was stupefied by the immediacy with which she accepted an invitation. So away he went on the appointed evening, was welcomed by the parents, and sat himself down. Up he jumped as he had been taught to do when he heard her coming down the stairs. When she came around the curve of the staircase he had no idea who she was because she was cheerless and plain, and one of her legs was in a brace. There followed what is known as the painful silence, or the awkward pause, while he gazed at her hopefully as if she and her treacherous parents might suddenly vanish and his problem be solved, for it had come to him at last that he had got the wrong girl. Without a word he walked to the door. But here he could not figure out the latch and then the crippled girl, half-dead with pity, limped to his side and showed him how."

Polajenko was standing across the room examining the contents of Allan Ehe's billfold. He did not seem to be listening.

"Three decades later he mentioned that evening. He could not forget what he had done because he knew in his heart that he was still capable of a similar act. Standing by my work bench he asked if I remembered, and when I said I did, he bitterly shook his bald head."

Polajenko folded a piece of paper into an airplane and

sent it gliding across the carpet where it landed beside the magazines. Tony unfolded it and read:

I long ago lost a hound, a bay horse, and a turtledove, and am still on their trail. Many are the travelers I have spoken to concerning them, describing their tracks and what calls they answered to. I have met one or two who had heard the hound and the tramp of the horse, and even seen the dove disappear behind a cloud, and they seemed as anxious to recover them as if they had lost them themselves.

"Thoreau," said Tony, who always read things that did not interest anyone else.

"From his wallet. Shall we study it under a microscope?"

"The typewriter is in his den and you can see the end of its carriage from where you are standing. If you don't believe me, turn around and look."

"If I didn't believe you, my friend, I would look," replied Polajenko. "I suppose you realize that certain people in this neighborhood are of the opinion you have two heads."

Tony answered with indifference. "I have a great deal to think about."

"Why is it you wear such formal clothes?"

"Why not?"

"But do you know anyone else who wears a frock coat and a top hat in the house?"

As if the inspector's question had disturbed him Tony took off the hat, looked it over, and finally put it back on his head. Polajenko continued to smoke in silence.

Once, scarcely loud enough to be heard, he asked, "Don't you symbolize something?"

And Miula answered, "Nothing whatsoever."

By this time Allan Ehe was on his journey to the morgue. His wife had been removed to the hospital in a catatonic state, and their four children were being fed by another neighbor.

"Altogether he was as fond of his wife as a man is apt to be of the one who substitutes for his genuine love, even though she was the most undistinguished woman who had ever aroused him. She was a devout Protestant named Winifred, a broad and tame creature with a hoarse voice and a detachable blonde coronet that framed her serene violet eyes. He had married her less than a month after being jilted by a thin, chilly little person who taught ballroom dancing."

Tony got up from the carpet like a giraffe, his eyes enormous with concern, and hurried into the kitchen. Presently he returned with two fragrant cups of coffee on a bamboo tray. Then, sitting down in his favorite position, he began a vague, wandering account of the year Ehe had spent in Greenwich Village, a year during which he fancied himself a poet.

"You see, my inspector, the idea came to him right after his elder brother died of leukemia, leaving behind a ten-thousand-dollar insurance policy. Allan flew de luxe to New York where he took a four-dollar-a-week room because he was of the opinion one must suffer in order to write poetry. While walking through the Village one rainy night, thinking how coarse people were, he happened to meet a Ukrainian girl named Natalie who also possessed a soul, so they began living together. They moved into a garret from which one could see a few yards of the Hudson providing there was not too much laundry on the lines, and there he wrote poetry while she decorated the walls

with spirals and cubes and odalisques, meanwhile telling
him about the slavery endured by women of the old
Ukrainian families. In turn he told her how much he disliked Illinois, except for squirrel hunting and the wiener
roasts on certain October evenings when the poplars and
oaks stood about in the smoky dusk in attitudes of grave
meditation. He never told her he had ten thousand dollars.

"They bought the worst available phonograph in a junk
shop and took it to her father who was a butcher in the
Bronx. The butcher was very good at mechanical things,
whereas Allan was an artist, and soon had the machine repaired so they returned to their garret and began playing
'Where the Bee Sucks There Suck I,' meanwhile making
a joke of everything that happened, no matter what.

"Her murals were rather muddy but as all their friends
were similar to themselves no one criticized this fact. In
the center of the attic hung a mobile which everyone admired and which turned idly around this way and that as
though keeping an eye on so much happiness. They drank
red wine and white wine at the proper times, looking
critically at the glasses, ate smoked cheese and crackers
and a great deal of spaghetti which Natalie cooked and
invariably said was not successful. Throughout the evening they would play with each other, calling one another
darling, and wandering about the garret holding hands.
Often she would curl up in his lap and twist a lock of his
hair around her fingers while their guests watched with
casual sophistication. He learned to tell jokes about how
naïve she had been when they began living together. Idly,
sipping the wine, he dissected her as though she were on
a table for everyone to enjoy, while she murmured in

mock embarrassment, 'Do stop, Randy,' which was the
name she had decided to call him.

"At about this stage they bought a dozen heavy white
porcelain mugs to replace the glasses. In this way everyone
could use two hands to drink the wine, meanwhile smiling
with relief at having escaped the world of the Philistines.

"Late at night they usually went for a walk beside the
river with their closest friends, a couple named Jones. This
couple was unable to get married because his previous wife
refused to divorce him, so she had gotten her last name
changed from Langendorf to Jones. They lived in a basement near Washington Square and if no trucks were
parked in the way they could see half of the arch. She
wrote free verse while he spent the day designing heroic
statuary."

"Tony! Tony, let me rest," begged Polajenko.

"Of course, Inspector. I'll tell it in the third person.
Tony visited Allan and Natalie. One evening, together
with a girl friend of Natalie's who was fond of saying she
would like to be a man, they went for a serious walk.
Through the smoke and grit and roaring automobiles they
sauntered, thinking what a fine thing it was to exist at
the center of the universe, and presently the girl, whose
name was Alec, became playful. She scooped up some
water from a fountain and threw it on Tony, clutched him
by the hand, and cried to the night, 'Why don't we run?'
Tony refused to run. Therefore she dashed back and forth
pulling up tufts of grass, pausing now and then to gaze
thoughtfully at the stars. When they sat on the concrete
revetment of the river she sat a little apart and with chin
cupped in her hands she looked mournfully across to Jer-

sey, as though she perceived more than neon lights and the omnipresent rumbling.

"With the candor of intimate friends Natalie inquired how much money silversmiths could make; Tony replied so brusquely that she was offended. Allan smiled dryly; he had not warned her about Tony. Alec soon inquired when he would be moving to New York and when he said he would not she looked at him in stupefaction. On their way home to the Village she walked beside him with extreme dignity, as though they were going down the aisle, but suddenly exclaimed, 'How do you expect me to write a book?' Natalie instantly cried, 'Oh, but you must! You have so much to say.' And Alec closed her eyes in pain, saying quietly, 'But I have not even closed a single episode. I must close an episode before I write my book.' Natalie shivered. 'I should feel intellectually naked afterwards.' There came an opening in the boulevard traffic; all four clutched hands and dashed to safety. The girls could not run very fast because they were wearing tight knickers.

"Some weeks after this evening Tony Miula, back among his metals and clippings, began to receive a series of incoherent letters from Allan. The letters told of going to a university psychiatrist, of envy and despair and most of all confusion. Natalie told him repeatedly that he was the greatest living poet in the English language, and to him at night she would whisper, 'You need me now. I'm the stronger.'

"Allan enclosed some lines he had written:

> In the day I have blamed you,
> In the night have I shamed you,
> Chill abbess I love.

"And that was mostly what his life in the Village consisted of. His poems were all very short and related to her. She was large and bony with luminous brown eyes like those of a nocturnal animal. He wrote of the gas that seeped into their garret from a broken pipe somewhere in the wall, and later, when they shared the basement with the Jones couple, of how clogged his head felt every morning.

"He wrote more and more often, until each mail brought two or three letters; then all at once when he was near to madness the clouds lifted for an instant that he might see himself on the cliff. The next day he left New York. Back home he spent week after week shuffling through the streets, and each afternoon he lay face down in the grass of the public square while the sun turned his neck as black as an old walnut. If anyone spoke to him he would begin to weep. Then one evening shortly before sundown he stood up, felt his jaw, and lurched across the square to a barber shop. The following week he had a job and was playing cards with his neighbors."

"Excuse me," said Inspector Polajenko, "but nobody behaves like that. Whose story is this? I seem to see not him but you as the poetaster."

Tony answered with a benign smile. "The point is that artistic garrets are full of people playing 'Where the Bee Sucks There Suck I.' Here is the land where this man was born and where he died. God give me to say what he suffered."

"I hate to seem stupid," said the inspector with a sigh, "but why is it you detour around honesty? You are verbal and clever enough, but your vision is perverse and astigmatic. All rays must converge at the retina, else we are lost." He stopped pacing the floor and stood a while gazing down on Tony, who met his look with equal strength.

"Actually, I respect you, Mr. Polajenko."

"Don't apologize when you say it. Do you know you look just like my brother?"

"But I *am* your brother."

"When you talk like that," Inspector Polajenko said grimly, "I can't understand a single word you say. You were telling me he went to a priest for advice. Go on."

There followed a long silence. Rain dripped steadily from the eaves.

At last Tony replied, "I never said that, but he did. He was told the Savior loved him."

"And what do you think of that?"

"It's all well enough provided a few mortals do too." He dipped his tongue into the cool coffee and closed his eyes. "Inspector, do you know, the first time you looked at me I knew a lot about you."

"To be understood is about the most fascinating thing I know," answered Polajenko. "But quite frankly, my friend, your assurance is irritating, particularly in one who understands the world not from practice but speculation. You sit astride it all with such disdain, a cavalier upon a nag. Come now, once in a while there must be empty bottles in your trash barrel."

Tony vigorously shook his head.

Polajenko examined the end of his cigar which he had chewed as flat as a paint brush.

"Just two things interested Allen as much as astronomy. One was a woman addicted to pornography, the other was building something. Still and all, each soul is a flower in the Master's bouquet."

"Please be lucid. Are you able to tell me what our subject did after he failed as a poet?"

"He operated an elevator. I often went downtown in order to ride in that elevator. Up and down we'd go. He had a beautiful speaking voice. One knew he believed he should have been a radio announcer. When calling the floors he modulated his tone and stood so erect. I would stand directly behind him and murmur, 'Your diction is superb. If I were a producer I would make you famous.' Such things do happen, you know; if they did not you would probably have more suicides than you have now. Good fortune, good fortune. It's like the truncated pencil sellers who deny their estate by hanging about their necks a placard which says, 'Keep Smiling.' Or the blind minstrels who quaver that happy days are here again.

"He did drink. Oh, how he drank! After a few he would become solemn and forthwith dispense his soul like a box of chocolates. Off he would go on business trips now and again, but always registered under an alias at a hotel with wooden walls. In his room he immediately took out his pen knife and began boring peepholes. He carried with him a role of adhesive tape to insure his own privacy when he so desired. Do you find him evil?"

Polajenko shrugged, his eyes returning casually to the scissors with which Tony was prying out staples.

"I, myself—" Tony continued, but here he belched, pressed a hand to his chest, and exclaimed, "Excuse *me!* Now I myself began as a thin child with wind-tossed hair and brilliant gypsy eyes, and did not fill my pockets with junk or go skating on the mill pond, so of course had I done the things Allan did the world would have brayed 'I told you so.' One of our instincts is to produce a play,

which is the reason he did not shoot himself in the bedroom, say, but yonder among the roses."

Polajenko's eyes fastened greedily on the gangling silversmith, while about his red lips there formed the trace of a
cynical smile.

"He gave the impression that he was living his life in
order to have done with it. He became interested in foods
and wines to pass the years away. Oh, he thought a good
bit, but he never had any worthwhile thoughts. Mostly he
brooded over women, and I grant you it sometimes does
appear that the world and all consists of anatomy and not
one stroke more. But with Plymouth obstinance we ignore
the nature of man, then look what you have! Why is everyone so astounded when a child is ravished?" Tony sat up
straight and began tapping his lips with his fingertips as
if trying to remember something.

"Oh, yes! He used to stand in corners with his arms
folded, if that tells you anything. And I would see him
walking in the garden holding lofty dialogues with himself. He felt that time was passing and he seemed vaguely
baffled and resentful of the fact, for he knew he had not
done much. He was commencing to grow old in the most
commonplace way. He attracted no notice. One thought of
him as aging, nothing more. He did not grow majestic, or
even confident. He just went down that road feeling bad,
do you understand? And he wasn't going to be treated—
oh, never mind, never mind." Tony looked gloomily at
the carpet. "Last year about this time I was awake before
dawn. I remember how the shadows lightened. On their
sleeping porch I saw his wife rolling about as if something
troubled her dreams. Her breasts poured heavily like flow-
ing batter around and around while he sat on the edge of

the bed glaring down at them as if his destiny were his death as well."

"Common enough," muttered Polajenko with a melancholy smile.

"That morning the bull was bellowing against his forehead. By some divining instinct he knew that life was happening to him. It was this knowledge he denied for so long in New York. There he grew a beard like an old-time Bolshevik; even so I remembered most clearly not the symbol of virility but his uneasy eyes, timid and frightened, of robin's-egg blue, or like those of a drowned man under water. I understood then about the ferocious beard, why he had grown it."

"I wish," said Polajenko wearily, "that you would put a hoop around each story so that I might gather them up."

"And you would like them labeled, too."

"That would make my job easier," Polajenko admitted. "Pardon me for saying this, but you're not quite real."

"That depends."

"You don't understand. What I say is that I never met anyone who acted like you. You don't talk like anybody I know. Furthermore you don't live the way people do."

"You just haven't watched closely," said Tony, getting to his feet. "By the way, did you count the cigarette stubs under the trellis? He smoked all night. What did you find in his bathrobe?"

"Chewing gum, a comb, and an empty match box. I find myself wondering if he would still be alive if he had found some more matches."

"So you conclude I am not a murderer after all!"

"Ah," said Polajenko with regret. "That is the trouble

with you. A person says a word and it echoes from you as a paragraph."

"Stop showing off to yourself."

Polajenko winked slyly, as though the two of them shared an agreeable secret.

"Is there anything else you want?" asked Tony with a rather stiff countenance.

"As a matter of fact, yes," said the inspector, "but I doubt if you will give it to me."

They stood a few seconds almost back to back. Tony Miura's eyes glittered ominously. "All right!" he burst out. "What is it? What is it?"

"Your scalp."

"Of course! You caught me that time. Why am I so stupid?" He slapped himself on the forehead.

The inspector turned around to gaze at him in mild surprise, and then looked down at the sallow, bony hands as if they confirmed something he had always suspected. Idly he said, "They tell me you are a great hunter."

"That's a lie!"

Polajenko peeled the cellophane from a smaller cigar and after licking one end he replied, "It is a lie and I am sorry. I'll never lie to you again. All the same, why don't you hunt? There is squirrel and quail in the woods just over the ridge. I often go there. Men are like that. They must kill a little or go insane from humiliation and despair. Why don't I meet you there sometime?"

"Then you accuse me!" He slapped himself again and announced to the ceiling, "Ah, God, that I should chop tiger hair for the gruel of an ass!"

Inspector Polajenko sighed wearily. "What a fellow you are! I don't see why we can't be friends."

"Shall I tell you? Because I'm smarter than the people you deal with—all the lonely bats and thugs. I may even be a watt brighter than you."

At this Polajenko stepped swiftly up to Tony Miula and pulled the horsy face down until it was touching his own. "Queer fish, I am going along with you," he whispered, threatening, then he stepped backward and blew a puff of smoke.

"You hurt my feelings," said Tony, rubbing his throat where Polajenko's powerful hand had caught him. "I won't tell you any more."

"Oh, really!" the inspector said in a good humor again. "Do you want me to give you the third degree?"

Tony looked petulant. "Your center of gravity is outside yourself. I thought you were more of a man, but you're just like Allan. Give you a push and down you go."

Polajenko groaned. "You exhaust me."

But Tony was already into a fresh narrative and as usual did not feel it necessary to connect one thought to the next, believing that anyone worth speaking to would contribute his own power. The incident took place at a country-club dance on New Year's Eve when Allan Ehe was twenty-two. He escorted to the celebration a girl no one there had ever seen, who at first was rumored to be a famous Continental beauty. However, the minute she opened her mouth it was obvious she came from some midwestern town enclosed by wheat sheaves, and in fact she turned out to be the niece of his sister-in-law up for a visit. But if her varnish had an apparent crack, Allan's had not. He danced around the floor once in a while with fearful dignity, disdaining all rhythm but the waltz, which meant they spent most of their time at their table, she a little baffled but trying to match his somber expression. Following each waltz he would lead her to the Louis Quatorze mirror, encircled by gold leaves and bucolic angels. There without a smile he would adjust his white necktie or pick lint from his lapel. Everyone watched him. He ignored his friends or bowed severely like a timid ambassador. He told no jokes; he relaxed not an instant. Never again in his life would he command such a gathering of people. He made only one mistake; he accepted an invitation to join a party. There the cardboard trumpets and paper hats did their appointed work, and when Tony all at once exploded a sack of confetti on his head he was destroyed, for his dignity was conscious.

"I caught up to him by the mirror," Tony continued. "He wasn't looking at himself this time, believe me. He was heading toward the safety of the men's room where he intended to lock himself in a cubicle. Frankly I had intended to finish him off but I saw he was dying and where is the sport of a *coup de grâce*? I enjoy the slaughter of Titans, but I do not shoot squirrels."

"Did you feel at ease with him?"

"I called him by his first name."

"I am not going to put up with you much longer."

Tony shrugged, as if to inquire what better the inspector had to do. "Analogies, like epigrams, are stronger in poetry than verity, all the same Allan Ehe was somewhat analogous to a spider that remains visible so long as it is not endangered, but retreats when assaulted. After his crucifixion at the country club he was not seen for almost a week." Tony plucked irritably at the carpet with his scissors and eventually admitted, "I had hoped right up to the last that he would learn something from me. He died for lack of strength. I saw the beastly gun drop from his hand into the wet grass. I saw the robins spring from the trees all around and fly off in alarm—"

"Pardon me, but how tall are you?"

"Six feet and seven inches. In the morning."

"Goodness!" exclaimed the inspector grimly. "That means we would be the same height if I should cut off your head. How tall are you at night?"

"Just a little shorter. During the day our cartilage is compressed."

"All the same," the inspector answered without much inflection, "most people don't find it necessary to mention such a fact. As for the robins you think you saw, they have no nests in that back yard. But go on, though Diogenes has passed you by."

"We were playing bridge on the train when a strange young woman hurried past. She was not much to look at but as she was alone he immediately began to follow her. Now he was handsome enough at twenty-six, though already showing a slight baldness and the ambitious belly of which he was so vain, for it signified success, and he loved to boast of his conquests, being of the opinion that I envied him. We followed her to a Pullman near the end of the train and there she sat down opposite two nuns who were amusing themselves with a game of string—"

Tony held up his hands to demonstrate how they had been weaving the string.

"—which is a good game to play for a few seconds, but the nuns played it by the hour. Frankly I was ashamed so I returned to the vestibule but he was undismayed; he sat down beside the quarry. He was a master of fatuity, even the crows would listen when he spoke. However he had some difficulty here and soon came back to the vestibule for a cigarette. I goaded him very well, I think; he swelled up like a toad but could not think of anything to say. So long as he succeeded at anything he could be taunted endlessly, responding with an imbecilic grin, but when he failed he lost his humor. I knew this but I continued because I always played the footman to this fat Don Juan and got a little tired of it. When he started to reach out the window in order to knock the ashes from his cigarette I was seized with hatred and struck the cigarette out of his hand—like that! The wind would have blown the ash into my face, at least I think it might have. I could have stepped backward as quickly as I slapped, but I did not and that was the point. Allan perceived in my action a rather cogent truth, which is that the illuminating act is the instinctive one, and in a fraction of a second may refute the manner of a lifetime. In this particular case it did not refute anything but simply stated in italics that I, of all persons, had never respected him. He was always tender as a scallion. The days of life we shared were sweet and rich for me. He never knew I sucked the very liquid of his soul. He did not learn a thing from me. Well, his death was not the first time I ate the bitter herb of heartbreak and neglect. Under a skylight in Greenwich Village I have been betrayed. When you have written the name of your love in the sand and presently watched the tide return, what more can you see?

"He spoke of suicide on dreary nights. Those who speak of it may do it, textbooks be damned. Once he came tapping on my door and handed me his will. He was a fraud that night, still I engaged him in a treasure hunt. I hid bits of tissue paper here and there and gave him the first instruction to open the dictionary at a certain page. There he found the second bit of tissue directing him to a picture on the wall, and behind this there was another telling him to peep under the sofa. From there he went to the icebox and from there to the medicine cabinet. Eventually, in the wastebasket, he found his will which I had torn in half. That is the way to do it, I said to him, let the policemen chase you a while."

"You know," said Polajenko with a bemused expression, "I'm sorry we gave the Salvation Army our iron maiden."

"But he loved her," Tony complained.

"Our rapport is breaking down, my friend. Whom are we talking about?"

"She fed him and kept him warm, woman's first concern for man."

Polajenko took off his glasses and pinched the bridge of his nose. "Are you talking about Natalie?"

"No, certainly not. I'm telling you about Winifred."

"I can't remember all these people."

But Tony was speaking at the same time. "Every Tuesday morning she goes into the back yard with a creaking wicker basket full of wet clothing and hangs it up to dry. I always hope for a windy morning; then the sheets pop like flags and the water runs down her forearms and drips from her plump elbows while she clips the washing to her line. I watch through the hedge more dead than alive, for she stands so—astride the basket—arms raised in triumph! Ah, that I might be a sculptor! The rope would go, to be sure, and the basket and the frock. But that all requires a noble mind. It suits me better to work with leather and chips of second-rate Mexican jade. But before I die I will hold one day in my hand a chisel, and I shall see beyond it an obelisk of marble from the quarries of Carrara, and no god known shall stop me. One day I will walk in Paradise. Now like a murdered actor do you look, in life's adroit facsimile of death! But I've no pennies to waste upon your eyes. . . ."

"I *have* been looking at you, it is true," replied Polajenko, "and now I know for the first time what it is has puzzled me. I have seen the shadows pass over your face, but did not know what they meant. It is not love itself you want or need, like other men, but only its image. If the curse of manhood had not dried up all my tears I think I could weep for you."

Struck by the inspector's tone Tony Miula hesitantly raised his eyes and found that Polajenko was looking at him with love, and a feeling long unfamiliar came into his heart as silently as the tide.

"Excuse me," said Polajenko, "but if you were awake and watching when the gun dropped from his hand then you must have seen him examine the weapon and raise it to his temple. Now if that is so, why did you allow it to happen? Or are you not your brother's keeper?"

"He had been lifting that gun for decades and it was my opinion that only he could lower it. I knew that something awful was happening to him, that some dread hour had come."

"I'm sorry, but that doesn't satisfy me."

"Well," Tony argued, "with the copious wisdom of hindsight I think next time I might do something about it. I might scream. However he was obstinate, as little men are apt to be, and having decided to shoot something he might as well have let go at me. Why don't you get out and leave me alone? I'm tired and have nothing more to say. Leave!"

Polajenko leaned backward in astonishment. But upon recovering from his surprise he recalled that he was not a guest to be ordered about; he grew angry and said he would leave when he pleased.

"But you are persecuting me," Tony whimpered.

"You! You sound an eerie chord, my friend, minor and foreign to the ear."

Before the last consonant had died away Tony's barbaric scissors whirled and flashed across the room, struck Polajenko flat on the breast and dropped almost reluctantly to the carpet. After a long silence during which the men looked away from each other Polajenko whispered, "You have thrown scissors before. . . . You could have hit me with both blades."

Tony nodded sullenly.

"That's enough," Polajenko muttered, buttoning up his raincoat.

"Yes or no?" said Tony. "Tell me if I am accused."

"Why should I tell you? You won't go anywhere." Polajenko began to grin. "Why, any time I want you I'll have you. I'll ring the bell and you'll hurry to let me in."

"I know things you will never learn from anyone else."

"But you garnish everything! Give you a pat of dough just large enough for a biscuit and you try to make a wedding cake." Polajenko considered the scissors which had stuck in the carpet. "Tony, you react like a woman. A man would have been careful not to alarm me."

Tony made a wry face. "It is easier to master desire than grief."

Polajenko grinned maliciously. "And some enjoy their guilt. Come now, you marionette, aren't you a little pleased he's dead?" Taking off his glasses again he began to squeeze his eyes. "It is easy to feel poetic about the tragedy of others. To know poetry when we ourselves have been victimized requires a peculiar mind."

"The sentiment is lovely, but I doubt the facts. The limbs of my neighbor are stiffening by the instant. Why don't you leave me?"

Polajenko sighed, as he had done from time to time, and made no attempt to answer, and his exhausted expression did not change, as though he were through with all struggling forever.

"The poles were established in the first act. For him the experience of others could not provide a solution. This garden so formal to the eye, who sees beneath the soil where roots go spiraling down in search of greater life, enfolding rocks, relics, or bones with indiscrimination, plunging through burrows in their hunger? His life was a feckless search for manhood.

"Do you know what caused him to fall in love? First of all it was her nose, which is long and bony. He would often feel of it in a kind of fascination and so she thought him quite strange indeed. Then one day he happened to toss her a pomegranate; she clutched, as women do, but managed to hang onto it. This surprised him. He had been prepared to laugh; instead he grew sober, looked at her in a melancholy way but said nothing. Later he alluded to the incident and she realized that somehow the fact that she had been able to catch a pomegranate had made him love her more than anything else she had ever done."

"Excuse me, but he seems to have told you a suspicious lot."

Tony looked at him in surprise. "But I collect stamps!"

The inspector considered this for a little while and finally said, "Ah, yes. So did he. Over stamps and wine rare confidence passes. Lord, I feel so unnecessary."

"But he never outgrew the insecurity of youth. It's a pleasure to be a little older and not so fearful of ridicule. But Allan went hunting like Ponce de León and his quest was the more stupid because he saw only the beds of various motels. That was when he sold automobiles. For two years he stood around rocking on his heels and gazing numbly at the floor or the ceiling, sometimes touching his bald spot or coughing gently into his fist. I would walk by the showroom and grimace; he would stare at me as through a mist of chloroform. He was just barely a success because, like all merchants worthy of the name, he was stupefied by anything that did not come with a set of directions. He did not know, nor did he care, that its name is Betelgeuse, or that it could annihilate the sun. But he spoke with authority; thus even when he was dead wrong few persons dared contradict him, for he sounded so right.

"He made excellent bait. There is nothing I would rather have for breakfast than the disposition of a bigot. One morning I strolled into the drugstore where he worked for a while. The instant he saw me he looked suspicious and uneasy. Strange—he never trusted me. I handed him a broken fountain pen. He said they were out of stock on that pen and wouldn't be getting repair parts. 'It's a hundred-year pen,' I said. 'Every part is guaranteed unconditionally for a hundred years.' He said, 'This par-

ticular model has been discontinued.' And I said, 'Then
what good is the guarantee?' He was furious, but finally
said he would give me another pen. I said I didn't want
another, I wanted this one fixed, and I waved the guarantee at him. You should have seen him. I told him he
should see a psychiatrist about that temper. The pen only
cost nineteen cents and I broke it deliberately, of course.
Allan suspected me right from the first. That night he
slipped into my garage and released the air from the tires
of my bicycle. Isn't that childish? He was a jealous and
greedy man, and every time I stung him he ran off waving
his arms and screaming."

Polajenko interrupted. "Now listen to me. Here is a
man felled like a tree. Something has cut him down. You
have shown me his branches, but where is the trunk? I
want something to grab hold of."

"You must be very nervous to constantly tug your mustache like that."

"Oh, that's nothing," muttered the inspector. "The only
thing that annoys me is I always pull the same side and
take out so much hair I look lopsided. Now where were
we? You're such a Pagliacci that you and your dead neighbor are inextricably tangled in my mind. In all you say
about him I seem to find you."

"If the nails the carpenter hammers form an interesting
pattern, is the carpenter responsible? When we are young
we value nothing we cannot eat or put into our pocket,
and when we are old if we value nothing more, there comes
a sorry end. So he fell in the summer house, above his
blind eyes an intricate lattice with its roses. I hear the
tramp of many feet. Look out the window there! See how
the trellis shakes? Mark this well. We are coming to break

ourselves a souvenir—a thorn or a blossom to remember him by. Yet time was, time is, time will be, so the Magi say. Allan lost three things. Are we not as anxious to recover them as if we had lost them ourselves?"

Polajenko had gone to the window while Tony remained cross-legged on the floor. In the next yard many people were standing about, gazing now at the police, now at the trellis where the wicker chair lay on its side, and as these people walked around they left their footprints in the wet and bending grass. One stooped, sudden as a hawk, having found a cigarette butt unguarded, and put it in his pocket.

Polajenko stood by the window a long time with his hands gripping the lapels of his raincoat, and finally he said, "Now you have told me an *avant-garde* story, you gadfly. I am not sure that I like it. I may think it over or I may presently cut off your head. How would you like that?" But he was burlesquing himself.

Tony smiled happily. "It is a waste of time to think, I assure you, my inspector, for whether we concern ourselves with a thousand hounds or a turtledove, the heart remains generalissimo."

Inspector Polajenko turned from the window with a shrug and passed out into the rain, and was never seen by the silversmith again.

Arcturus

Verweile doch, du bist so schön.
Linger awhile, thou art so fair.
—GOETHE

The children, Otto and Donna, have been allowed to stay
up late this evening in order to see the company. Now
with faces bewitched they sit on the carpet in front of the
fireplace, their pajama-clad legs straight out in front of
them and the tails of their bathrobes trailing behind so
that they look somewhat like the sorcerer's apprentice.

Outside the wind is blowing and every once in a while
the window panes turn white; then the wind veers and the
snow must go along with it. Automobile horns sound quite
distant even when close by. Aside from the hissing, sputter-
ing logs which are growing black in the fire, and the allur-
ing noises of the kitchen, the most noticeable sound is a
melancholy humming from the front door. Otto and
Donna are convinced a ghost makes this dreadful wailing
and no amount of explanation can disprove it. Their father has lifted them up one after the other so that they
can see it is only a piece of tin weather stripping that vi-
brates when the wind comes from a certain direction, and

they have felt a draft when this happens, but their eyes
are dubious; wind and metal are all very well but the
noise is made by a ghost. It is a terrible sound, as no one
can deny, and upon hearing it Otto shivers so deliciously
that his little sister must also shiver.

"What does company look like?" he inquires without
lifting his gaze from the burning logs. And is told that
company will be a gentleman named Mr. Kirk. Otto considers this for a long time, wiggling his feet and rubbing
his nose which has begun to itch from the heat.

"Is he coming to our house?"

Otto's father does not answer. Lost in meditation he sits
in his appointed chair beside the bookcase.

Presently Otto sniffles and wishes to know why the man
is coming here.

"To visit with your mother."

A cloud of snowflakes leaps to the window as if to see
what is going on inside but is frightened away by the
weather stripping. How warm the living room is! Donna
yawns, and since whatever one does the other must also do,
her brother manages an even larger yawn. The difference
is in what follows: Donna, being a woman, does not mind
succumbing, and, filled with security, she begins to lean
against Otto, but he is convinced that sleep is his enemy
and so he remains bolt upright with a stupidly militant
expression that tends to weaken only after his eyes have
shut. Though his enemy is a colossal one he accepts without concern the additional burden of his infant sister.

"Why?" he asks, and looks startled by his own voice. It
is doubtful he can now remember what he wishes to know,
but why is always a good solid question and sure to get
some kind of response.

"Because your mother wrote him a letter and begged him to come see her."

Again follows a silence. The clock on the mantel ticks away while the good logs crackle and the coals hiss whenever the sap drips down upon them. Otto is remotely troubled. For several weeks he has sensed that something is wrong in the house but he cannot find out what. His mother does not seem to know, nor does the cook, who usually knows everything. Otto has about concluded the nurse is to blame; therefore he does whatever she tells him not to do. Sometimes he finds it necessary to look at his father, or to sit on his lap; there, although they may not speak to one another, he feels more confident. He is jealous of this position and should Donna attempt to share in it he is prone to fend her off until orders come from above.

In regard to this evening, Otto has already gotten what he wanted. He does not really care about Mr. Kirk because the value of a visitor lies simply in the uses to which Otto can put him, whether it be staying up late or eating an extra sweet. All at once Donna topples luxuriously into his lap. His hand comes to rest on her tiny birdlike shoulder, but through convenience only. At the moment he is careless of the virgin beauty; her grace does not intrigue him, nor does he realize how this tableau has touched the heart of his father across the room. Somberly Otto frowns into the fire; almost adult he is in the strength of such concentration, though one could not tell whether he is mulling over the past or the future. Perhaps if the truth were known he is only seeing how long he can roast his feet, which are practically touching a log.

"Is he coming *tonight?*" Otto knows full well this is a foolish question, but there lurks the fear that if he does not show a profound and tenacious interest in the whole business he will be sent to bed.

With ominous significance his father demands, "Why do you think you two are up this late?"

Otto stares harder than ever into the fire. It is important now that he think up something to change the subject in a hurry. He yawns again, and discovers that he is lying down. He sits up. He inquires plaintively if he may have the drumstick on Christmas.

His father does not reply, or even hear, but gazes at the carpet with a faraway expression somewhere between misery and resignation and does not even know he has been spoken to by the cook until she firmly calls him by name.

"Mr. Muhlbach!"

He starts up, somewhat embarrassed. Cook wishes to know at what time the guest will be arriving. Muhlbach subsides a little, takes a sip from a tumbler of brandy, and is vague. "Ah . . . we don't know exactly. Soon, I hope. Is there anything you want?"

But there is nothing; she has finished all preparation for the dinner and now is simply anxious for fear that one delicacy or another may lose its flavor from so much waiting. She looks at the children on the carpet before the fireplace. Otto catches this look; he reads in cook's stern face the thought that if she were their mother she would have them in bed; instantly he looks away from her and sits quite still in hopes that both his father and the cook will forget he is even there. Seconds pass. Nothing is said. Cook returns to the kitchen with an air of disgust.

Now the suburban living room is tranquil once again, much more so than it was two hours ago. At that time

there were tears and reprimands and bitter injustice, or so
the participants think. Otto especially felt himself abused;
he was the object of an overwhelming lecture. He did not
comprehend very much of it but there could be no mistake
about who was in disgrace; therefore he rolled over onto
his stomach and began to sob. Surely this would restore
him to the family circle. No one, he thought, could refuse
to comfort such a small boy. It was a fine performance and
failed only because he peeked up to see its effect; at this
he was suddenly plucked from the floor by one foot. He
hung upside down for a while, gravely insulted, but found
it impossible to weep effectively when the tears streamed
up his forehead, so after a fit of coughing and bellowing he
was lowered to the carpet. On his head, to be sure, but
down at any rate, and for some time after he occupied himself with the hiccups. He still believes that his punishment
was not only too stringent but too prompt; one appreciates
a few moments in which to enjoy the fruit of one's evil-
doing. Furthermore all he did was take a stuffed giraffe
from his sister. It is true the giraffe belonged to him; the
trouble came about because he had not thought of playing
with the giraffe until he discovered she had it, and when
he had wrung it away from her he put it on the table out
of her reach. So, following the administration of justice,
he was ordered to kiss his little sister on the lips, a penance
he performs with monstrous apathy, after which the living
room was turned into a manger for perhaps the twentieth
time and the father magically transformed himself into
a savage dog, growling and snarling, keeping everything
for himself. Donna and Otto are spellbound, so terrifying
is their father in the role of a dog. In fact he is so menacing
and guards the cushions and pillows with such ferocity that

the point of the fable is invariably lost. On occasion they have even requested him to be a dog so that they might admire his fangs and listen enraptured to the dreadful growls. But perhaps they are learning, who can tell?

Now the lesson is ended and, as usual, forgotten. The giraffe is clamped upside down beneath Donna's lower arm; it is fortunate in having such a flexible neck. She no longer cares that a visitor is on the way; she does not listen for the doorbell, nor does she anticipate the excitement that is bound to follow. By firelight her hair seems a golden cobweb, an altogether proper crown. Blissfully asleep she lies despite the fact that her pillow is one of Otto's inhospitable knees. Barely parted and moist are the elfin lips, while her breath, as sweet as that of a pony, sometimes catches between them, perhaps betokening a marvelous dream. She cannot be true, Botticelli must have painted her. Her expression is utterly pious; no doubt she has forgotten her miniature crimes. One hopes she has not dwelt too hard upon those miniature punishments which followed.

Now comes a stamping of feet just outside, an instant of silence, and next the doorbell, dissonant and startling even when one expects it. Company is here! Otto is first to the door but there, overcome by shyness, allows his father to catch up and to open the door.

Here is more company than expected. Kirk has brought along someone he introduces as Miss Dee Borowski, an exotic little creature not a very great deal larger than Otto although she is perhaps eighteen. One knows instinctively that she is a dancer. She is lean and cadaverous as a greyhound, and her hair has been dyed so black that the highlights look blue. She draws it back with utmost severity,

twists it into a knot, and what is left over follows her with
a flagrant bounce.

They have entered the Muhlbach home, Sandy Kirk
tall as a flagpole and a trifle too dignified as though he will
be called upon to defend his camel's hair overcoat and
pearl-gray homburg. He has brought gifts: perfume for the
woman he is to visit, its decanter a crystalline spiral. For
the master of the house something more substantial, a bottle of high hard Portuguese wine. With a flourish and a
mock bow he presents them both to Muhlbach. He apologizes for his lateness by a rather elaborate description of
the traffic in the Hudson tube, and as if a further apology
may bring a smile of pardon to Muhlbach's face he adds
in an almost supplicating way that Borowski was late getting out of rehearsal. Immediately the dancer confesses
that her part will be small; she is third paramour in a
ballet production of "Don Juan." Well, she is feral enough
and will probably mean bad dreams for the young men in
the audience, but there is something ambivalent about her
as though she has not quite decided what to make of her
life. Her eyebrows, for example, do not grow from the
bony ridge that protects the eye; someone has plucked the
outer hairs and substituted theater brows that resemble
wings. She pauses beside the lamp and a shadow becomes
visible high on her forehead—it has been shaved. Now
she has decided to take off her new mink jacket; underneath is a lavender sweater that clearly intends to molt on
the furniture, and a pair of frosty-looking tailored slacks.
Quite rococo she looks, and knows it too. But to complete
this ensemble she is carrying a book of philosophy.

Replies Muhlbach, conscious that his own voice must
be a monotone, "My wife is upstairs. She will be down in

a few moments. This is our son and there asleep by the fire is Donna."

Kirk has been waiting for this introduction because he has presents for the children too. To Otto goes a queer little stick-and-ball affair, a game of some description. Otto receives the device without enthusiasm but minds his manners enough to say thank you. For Donna there is the most fragile, translucent doll ever seen. It is not meant for her to play with of course, being made of Dresden china, not for years yet. Kirk places it on the mantel.

Miss Borowski has stooped a little so that she and young Otto look at one another as equals. Otto wishes to appear self-sufficient but despite himself he likes what he sees; then, too, she is considerably more fragrant than his mother, who always has an odor of medicine. He decides to accept the overture. They are friends in an instant and together, hand in hand, they go over to inspect Donna, who has found the carpet no less agreeable than her brother's leg. Otto does not object to anyone's admiring his baby sister; there are times when he discovers himself seized by the desire to tickle her ribs or her feet. He does not know this is love. So much the better, for if he knew he might stop. Nor is he unaware that she is the beauty of the house, though he takes comfort in the memory of her astonishing helplessness. He fails to understand why, despite his instructions, she cannot learn to put on her own shoes or even go to the toilet when necessary.

Sandy Kirk meanwhile has been appraising the home and he has learned something: the supper table has been set. Only then does he recall the invitation was for supper. Unfortunately he and the dancer stopped to eat before coming over. Muhlbach hands him a cocktail, which he accepts with a serene smile; he waits to see if there will be a toast, but there is none. He notes that Borowski is giving the little boy a taste of her drink and he sees that Muhlbach frowns at this.

Into the room, supported by a nurse, comes Joyce Muhlbach, and the attention of everyone turns to her. She is unsmiling, clearly suffering deep pain. She is dressed but there is about her the look and the fetid odor of someone who has been in bedclothes all day. Her eyes are febrile, much too luminous. Straight across the room she moves, clutching the nurse's elbow, until she is in front of the invited guest. Kirk, in the midst of tapping a foreign cigarette on the back of his wrist, seems paralyzed by the sight of her. Her husband turns around to the fire and begins to push at a log with his foot. And the dancer, who is holding Otto by the hand, stands flat-footed with the prearranged expression of one who has been told what to expect; even so her greedy stare indicates that she is fascinated by the sick woman's appearance.

Joyce now stands alone, and while looking up at Kirk she addresses her son. "Isn't it about time for little boys to be in bed?"

Otto assumes that nasal whine which he feels the best possible for all forms of protest, but he knows the end has come. Still a token argument is necessary. He knows they expect one. He reminds his mother that he has been given permission to stay up tonight; the fact that it was she who gave the permission seems not especially cogent. With strangers present his pride forbids the wheedling and disgraceful clowning which is sometimes successful, so he is reduced to an obstinate monologue. His father picks up Donna, who is quite unconscious; she could be dragged upstairs and would not know the difference. All of a sudden Otto gets up from the corner where he has been stubbornly crouching since bed was mentioned, and the churlish whine disappears. He owns a rifle. It is on the top shelf of the hall closet where he cannot reach it; all the same it belongs to him, and if Miss Borowski has a fancy for rifles his father might bring it out. Otto has reasoned no further than this, indeed has done nothing but look crafty, when his father remarks that there will be no showing of the gun tonight. Otto instantly beseeches his mother, whom he considers the more sympathetic, and while his back is turned he feels himself caught around the waist by that inexorable arm he knows so well. His head goes down, his feet go up, and thus robbed of dignity he vanishes for the night.

There follows one of those queer instants when everything becomes awkward. Otto has taken away more than himself. Is it affectation that causes Dee Borowski to sit cross-legged on the floor? Time is running out on them all.

Joyce begins: "Well, Sandy, I see you got here."

The moments which follow are stark and cheerless despite the comfortable fire. A flippant answer could make things worse. One listens moodily to the poltergeist in the door. But Muhlbach re-enters to save them, re-enters briskly with a cocktail shaker and says, while filling the dancer's glass, "A month ago my father died." And he proceeds to tell about the death of young Otto's grandfather. Nothing about Muhlbach suggests the poet—certainly not his business suit, not his dictaphonic sentences, least of all his treasury of clichés. His story unwinds like ticker tape, yet the visitors cannot listen hard enough. Even Borowski has forgotten the drama of herself, and if one should quietly ask her name she might reply without thinking that it is Deborah Burns.

And the urbane Sandy Kirk, who has found his way around half the world, by this recital of degeneration and dissolution he drifts gradually into the past, into profound memories of his own. Unlike the ingénue, death is not unfamiliar to him, death is not something one mimes on cue; Kirk once or twice has seen it look him sharply in the eye and finds he does not care for that look. As the story progresses he begins to empathize with Muhlbach; he is gratified that this man does know some emotion, and he wonders less why Joyce married him. When he read her letter, read the sardonic description of her husband, he was astonished to perceive that beneath the surface she was utterly in love with the man, a man who until now has seemed to Kirk like a shadow on the water. He did not much want to come for this visit because he is afraid of Joyce. Their relationship never brought them any kind of fulfillment, never carried them to an ocean, as it were, but left them stranded in the backwash of lost opportunity. No matter how many years have since intervened she has had the freedom of his heart as now it seems he has had hers. Kirk has not been able to resolve his feelings about Joyce; he was never able to place a little statue of her in his gallery as he does with other women. No, the letter put him ill at ease; he did not want to see her ever again but there was in her appeal such urgency that he could not refuse. However, he has come prepared. He has thought everything out. He has brought along this terribly serious little ballerina for protection. He has only to say the magic word, that is, he need only mention ballet or the theater and Dee Borowski will take over, destroying all intimacy without ever knowing what she has done. It is a shrewd device, one Sandy Kirk has used in other clumsy situations; all the same he knows that Joyce will not be deceived.

Now Muhlbach, seated like the good merchant that he is, shaking up his trousers so as not to result in a bulge at the knee, continues in his oddly haunting style, telling how young Otto was invited to the sickroom but was not informed he would never see his grandfather again. And they talked a little while, did the boy and the old gentleman who was dying; they talked solemnly about what Otto had been doing that afternoon. In company with two other neighborhood gangsters he had been digging up worms. At the end of this conversation Otto received a present all wrapped up in Christmas tissue, though Christmas had hardly come into sight. It turned out to be a primer of archaeology, and while Otto held this book in his hands there beside the bed his grandfather sleepily explained that it was a book about the stars. After a momentary hesitation Otto thanked him. Muhlbach, standing on the other side of the deathbed, was carefully watching his son, and many times since that afternoon he has mulled over a very curious fact, the fact that Otto could recognize the word "archaeology" and knew its meaning. Indeed the book had been chosen for him because he had sounded interested in the subject; furthermore Otto has always had fewer qualms than a Turk about displaying his accomplishments. What restrained him from correcting his grandfather? It was a marvelous opportunity to show off. The father does not know for sure, but he does know that the boy is preparing to leave the world of childhood.

And so Muhlbach, without understanding exactly why

either of them did what they did, hurried out to buy his son a rifle. In a sporting-goods store he handled the light guns one after another, slipped the bolt and examined the chamber, raised the sights, caressed the stock, and in fact could hardly contain his rapture, for he has always been in love with guns. To one side stood the clerk with arms folded and a mysterious nodding smile. "This is a twenty-two, isn't it?" Muhlbach asked, though naturally it was not a question but a statement. However he bought no ammunition because even pride must genuflect to reason.

From the bedroom comes the querulous voice of Otto, who has been abandoned, and he wishes to know what they are talking about.

"Go to sleep!" orders his father.

In the bedroom there is silence.

Every few minutes the cook has peered out of the kitchen, not to see what is going on but to announce her impatience. She has allowed the door to swing back and forth; she has rattled silverware and clinked glasses. She cannot figure out why people linger so long over a drink. She herself would drink it down and be done with the matter.

Kirk is now obliged to confess that both he and the dancer have eaten. Pretense would be impossible. He turns helplessly to Joyce with his apology and she feels a familiar annoyance: it is all so characteristic of him, the tardiness, the additional guest, the blithe lack of consideration. How well she remembers this selfish, provoking man who means so much to her. She knows him with greater assurance than she can ever know her deliberate and, in fact, rather mystic husband. She remembers the many nights and the

mornings with a tenderness she has never felt toward
Muhlbach. Thus Sandy Kirk finds her appraising him and
he glances uneasily toward her husband: Muhlbach is ab-
sorbed by the snow clinging to the window panes.

It is decided that the guests shall sit at the table and
drink coffee while dinner is served the host and hostess;
there is no other solution. And they will all have dessert
together. The cook thinks this very queer and each time
she is summoned to the dining room she manages a good
bourgeois look at the ballerina.

Around the mahogany oval they sit for quite a long
time, Muhlbach the only one with an appetite. Once Joyce
Muhlbach lifts her feverish gaze to the ceiling because the
children's bedroom is just overhead and she has heard
something too faint for anyone else, but it was not a significant noise and soon she resumes listening to Sandy
Kirk, who is describing life in Geneva. He says there is a
tremendous fountain like a geyser in the lake, and from
the terrace of the casino it is one of the most compelling
sights in the world. Presently he tells about Lausanne farther up the lake, its old-world streets rising steeply above
the water, and from there he takes everyone in seven-
league boots to Berne, and on to Interlaken where the
Jungfrau is impossible to believe even if you are standing
in its shadow.

Muhlbach clears his throat. "You are probably not
aware of the fact, but my parents were born in Zurich. I
can recall them speaking of the good times they used to
have there." And he goes on to tell about one or two of
these good times. They sound very dull as he gives them,
owing in part to his habit of pausing midway to cut, chew,
and swallow some roast beef. It occurs to him that Kirk

may speak German so he asks the simplest question,
"Sprechen sie Deutsch?" Conversation in German affords
him a kind of nourishment, much the same as his customary evening walk around the block, but aside from his
mother, who now lives in an upstate sanatorium, there is
no one to speak it with him. Joyce has never cared much
for the language and it appears that Otto will grow up
with a limited vocabulary.

Kirk replies, *"Nein. Spanisch und Französisch und
Italienisch."* To Kirk the abrupt question was disconcert-
ing because he had fancied himself the only one capable
of anything beyond English. He has come to this home
with the expectation of meeting a deadly familiar type of
man, a competent merchant who habitually locked his
brain at five o'clock, and Kirk is trying to remain convinced that this is the case. Muhlbach admits to not having
traveled anywhere dangerously far from the commuter's
line, south of Washington, say, or west of Niagara, and it
is one of Sandy Kirk's prime theses that a stay-at-home
entertains a meager form of life. The world, as anyone
knows, was made to be lived in, and to remain in one
place means that you are going to miss what is happening
somewhere else. All the same Kirk sports a few doubts
about his philosophy and so he occasionally finds it reas-
suring to convince other people that he is right. He has a
talent for evocation and will often act out his stories, tip-
toeing across the room and peering this way and that as
though he were negotiating the Casbah with a bulging wallet. Or he will mimic an Italian policeman beating his
breast and slapping his forehead over the criminal audac-
ity of a pedestrian. Very droll does Sandy Kirk become
after a suitable drink; then one must forgive his manifold

weaknesses, one must recognize the farcical side of life. Thus he is popular wherever he goes; it is a rare hostess who can manage to stay exasperated with him all evening.

He seems to present the same personality no matter what the situation: always he has just done something wrong and is contrite. He telephones at a quarter of eight to explain that he will be a little late to some eight o'clock engagement. "Well, where are you now?" they ask, because his voice sounds rather distant, and it turns out he is calling from another city. But he is there by midnight and has brought an orchid to expiate the sin. Naturally the hostess is furious and wishes him to understand he cannot escape so easily but her cutting stare is quite in vain because he can no more be wounded than he can be reformed. One accepts him as he is, or not at all.

Now he has taken them through the Prado, pausing an instant in the gloom-filled upper chambers where Goya's dread etchings mock the very earth, gone on to Fez and Constantine and swiftly brought them back to Venice, where a proper British girl is being followed by a persistent Italian. She will have nothing to do with this Italian, will not speak to him, nor so much as admit he lives, despite the most audible and most extraordinary invitations. Now a man must maintain his self-respect, observes Kirk with a dignified wink, so all at once the frustrated Italian seizes her and flings her into the Grand Canal, and wrapping his coat like a Renaissance cloak around his shoulders he strides regally off into the night. Such are the stories he tells in any of a hundred accents, and no one can be certain where truth and fiction amalgamate, least of all the narrator. He speaks incessantly of where he has been, what he has done, and the marvels he has seen. Oh, he is a character—so exclaims everyone who knows him. It is amazing that such a façade can exist in front of a dead serious career, but he is a minor official of the State Department and puzzles everyone by mumbling in a lugubrious way that his job is expendable and when the next election comes around they may look for him selling apples on the corner. Still, he travels here and there and draws his pay, rather good pay, no matter who is elected. It is suspected that he is quite brilliant, but if so he never gives any evidence of it: one second he is a perfect handbook of slang, the next he becomes impossibly punctilious. It is difficult to decide whether he is burlesquing himself or his listeners.

The Muhlbachs are content to listen, regardless, because there is little enough drama at home and this visitor floats about like a trade wind of sorts, bearing a suggestion of incense and the echo of Arab cymbals. His wallet came from Florence—"a little shop not far from the Uffizi," he will answer—and his shoes were made in Stockholm. They can hardly equal his fables by telling how sick young Otto was the previous summer even though he spent several weeks in a hospital bed and required transfusions. It was a blood disease and they were fortunate that one of Muhlbach's business partners had contracted the same thing as a child and could supply the antitoxin.

Nor can they explain the curious pathos everyone felt over a situation the doctor created. It happened on the worst day of the illness, when they had at last come to believe he could not get well. While the doctor was examining him Otto became conscious, and to divert him the doctor asked how he would like to attend the circus that evening. Otto thought that would be fine and managed enough strength to nod. So they agreed that the doctor should call for him at six o'clock sharp that they might have time to reach the grounds ahead of the crowd and secure the best possible seats. Otto then relapsed into a coma from which he was not supposed to recover, but one eye opened around five o'clock in the afternoon and he spoke with absolute lucidity, asking what time it was. There could be no doubt that the speaker must be either Otto or his reincarnation because he has always been fearfully concerned over the time. By five-thirty he was certain he should be getting dressed and by six o'clock he had begun to sob with frustration because the nurse prevented him from sitting up. When they sought to pacify him by means of a teaspoonful of ice cream he exclaimed "No" with pitiful violence. His father's promise of a trike when he got well was received with an irritated hiccup. In vain did they explain that the doctor had been teasing; Otto knew better. Any moment the door would open and they would all be dumbfounded. The clock ticked along, Otto watching desperately. The hand moved down and started up, and finally started down again. Then he knew for the first time those pangs that come after one has been lied to.

But perhaps it was not unjustified; they had thought he would leave them and he did not, and scars on a heart are seldom seen.

Meanwhile the cook has been acting superior. Around the table she walks and pours fresh coffee with her nose in the air as though its fragrance were offensive. She stumbles against Miss Borowski's chair, does this sure-footed cook. What can the matter be? And she is so careless in pouring that it slops over the cup into the saucer. It is true the cook apologizes, but her resentment is implicit and there follows a baffled silence at the table.

Joyce Muhlbach perceives the cause. Now it is clear. The cook is jealous of the ballerina. But who can imagine the cook in tights? It would take two partners to lift her. Here is an amiable creature shaped like a seal, beloved of her employers and playing Olympian roles to a respectful audience of Otto and Donna, yet unhappy. She has found a soubrette at her master's table and is bursting with spite. She too would be carried across a stage and wear mascara. Rather great tragedies may be enacted in the secrecy of the heart; at this moment something very like a tear is shining in the cook's artless eye.

Joyce again is listening to a sound upstairs. She is attuned to nothing with such delicacy as to the events of the nursery. Donna will cough only once, muffled by the pillow, yet her mother hears, and considers the import. Is it the cough of incipient disease, or nothing but the uncertain functioning of babyhood? Accordingly she acts. To her husband everything sounds approximately the same, but that is the way with husbands, who notice everything a little late. Good man that he is, he cannot even learn how to tell a joke, but must always preface it with a hearty laugh and the advice that his listeners had better get set to split their sides. Of course it is all one can do to smile politely when Muhlbach, after ten minutes of chuckling and back-tracking and clearing his throat, gets around to the point. Kirk would tell it with a fumbled phrase and be midway through another tale before his audience caught up with the first one.

She surveys them both as though from a great distance and knows that she loves them both, her husband because he needs her love, and Kirk because he does not. She half-hears the dancer asking if Sandy has changed since she knew him.

Again comes a stamping on the walk outside, but heavier than were the feet of Kirk. This is the sound of big men thumping snow from their boots. Everyone hears and looks through the archway toward the front door—that is, everyone except Joyce, who has instantly looked at her husband. Kirk from the corner of his eye has taken in this fact and for the first time becomes aware of the strength of this marriage: no matter what happens she will look first of all at her husband and react according to him. There is something old and legendary about this instinct of hers, something which has to do with trust. Kirk feels a clutch of envy at his heart; when he and she were together she did not necessarily look to him whenever anything happened; he had always thought her totally self-sufficient. Now Muhlbach turns back to the table, frowning, and considers his wife, but when she cannot supply the answer he crumples his napkin, places it alongside his plate, and goes to the door. They hear him open the peephole, call someone by name, and immediately swing open the door.

Cold and huge they come in, two men. Duck hunters they are. One is John Grimes and the other is always referred to as "Uncle." Muhlbach, appearing overjoyed, insists that they come into the dining room, so after a few minutes they do, though "Uncle" is reluctant. Both men are dressed in corduroy and heavy canvas. Grimes also wears a brilliant crimson mackinaw to which a few flakes of snow are clinging, and while he stands there boldly grinning the snow melts and begins to drip from the edges of his mackinaw onto the dining-room carpet. His pockets bulge with shotgun shells. His gigantic hands are swollen and split from the weather.

Behind him, away from the circle of light, stands Uncle, who is long and solemn and bent like a tree in the wind. His canvas jacket is open, revealing a murderous sheath knife at the belt; its hilt looks bloody. Dangling by a frayed strap over one of his bony shoulders is a wicker fishing creel, exhausted through years of use, from which a few yellowed weeds poke out. He has a bad cold and attends to it by snuffling every few seconds, or by wiping his nose on the back of his hand. Obviously he is more accustomed to kitchens than to dining rooms, nor would he seem out of place in overalls testifying at a revival. He grins and grins, quite foolishly, exposing teeth like crooked tombstones, and when he speaks there is always the feeling that he is about to say something bawdy. But he is considered a great hunter; it is a rare animal or bird that can escape from Uncle. At present he is gaping at Miss Borowski. Uncle recognizes her as an unfamiliar piece of goods but is not altogether certain what. Borowski returns the stare with contempt.

Both hunters smell acrid and salty. About them wells a devastating aboriginal perfume of wood smoke, fish, the blood of ducks, tobacco, wet canvas, beer, and the perspiration of three inchoate weeks. Sandy Kirk got up slowly when they came in. No longer the center of attention, he stands with his napkin loosely in one hand and watches what goes on, making no attempt to join the bantering conversation. Astutely he measures John Grimes. With one glance he has read Uncle's book but this Grimes is anomalous: he might be a politician or a lawyer or some

kind of professional strong man. Above all this duck
hunter is masculine. The cumbersome mackinaw rides
as lightly on him as does the angora sweater on Borowski.
His very presence has subtly dictated the terms of the as-
sembly: he rejects the status of guest and demands that
he be distinguished primarily as a man; therefore Joyce
and the dancer are necessarily reduced to being women.
By way of emphasis there looms behind him that sullen
scarecrow known as Uncle with a few whiskers curling under his chin, in his awkwardness equally male.

The duck hunter feels himself scrutinized and swiftly
turns his head to confront Sandy Kirk. For an instant they
gaze at each other without pretense; then they are civi-
lized and exchange nods, whereupon the hunter smiles
confidently. Kirk frowns a little. Whirling around, Grimes
makes a playful snatch at Uncle's chin as if to grab him by
the whiskers. "Try to kill me, will you?" says he, and turns
up the collar of the mackinaw to display a tiny black hole
caused by a shot. At this Uncle begins to paw the floor
and to protest but at that moment is petrified by an on-
coming sneeze which doubles him up as though Grimes
had punched him in the stomach. He emerges with a red
beak and watery eyes and begins hunting through his filthy
jacket for a handkerchief, which turns out to be the size
of a bandanna.

John Grimes snorts and grins hugely, saying, "Missed
the duck too!" This further mortifies Uncle. The two of
them look as though they can hardly restrain their spirits
after three weeks in the forest and may suddenly begin
wrestling on the carpet.

The cook has pushed open the kitchen door and is having a necessary look. Everyone is aware of her; she is not

subtle about anything. She seems particularly struck by the fact that both men are wearing knitted woolen caps— John Grimes' is black as chimney soot and Uncle's is a discolored turtle green. It is curious what a cap will do. A cap is like a beret in that when you see someone wearing it you can hardly keep from staring. Cook has seen these men dozens of times but looks from one to the other in stupefaction. She is not unjustified because the headgear causes Uncle to appear even taller and skinnier and more despondent than he is; if ever he straightens up, the pompom of his cap must certainly scrape the ceiling. At last, conscious that she herself is beginning to attract attention, though she knows not why, cook allows the kitchen door to close.

But another rubberneck is discovered. Near the top of the stairs a pinched white face looks through the railing, and of course it is Otto come out to see what this is all about. He resembles a lemur clutching the bars of some unusual cage, or a tarsier perhaps, with his impossibly large ears and eyes wide open for nocturnal prowling. Like the cook, Otto finds himself on display; he becomes defensive and starts to back out of sight, but is asked what he thinks he is doing up there.

"I want a drink," says Otto piteously, and quite automatically. He has been on the stairs for ten minutes listening without comprehension to a description of the camp in the forest. He comes part way downstairs, holding on to the banister, and as the chandelier light falls upon him it may be seen that if there is anything on earth he does not need it is a drink: his belly is so distended with water that the front of his pajamas has popped open; however, he appears to feel no draft. Unconscious of his ribald figure he asks, "Who are all those men?" He cares who they are, more or less, but the main thing is to turn the conversation upon someone else. While his mother is buttoning up his front he is trenchantly introduced to the hunters.

"Are they company?"

They are. The lack of repartee following his question implies he is unpopular, but Otto scintillates.

"What are they *doing?*"

It should be clear to anyone that the hunters are standing at the mahogany sideboard where the good cook has poured them each a cup of coffee. They are too wet to sit down anywhere. Otto studies them from top to bottom and says he thinks Donna needs to go to the toilet. Will someone come upstairs and see? The nurse is upstairs. If either of them needs anything the nurse will be aware of it. Otto feels the balance of power swinging away from him; unfortunately he cannot think of anything to say, anything at all. He stands on the bottom step with his belly out like a cantaloupe and those dark eyes—the gift of his mother —wondering. There is nothing special on his mind when he complains that he wants to see the ducks; in fact he hardly knows what he said and is startled that it has gotten a reaction.

Grimes and Uncle have bagged a few over their legal limit, to be sure, but that is not the reason they have brought some to the Muhlbachs. At any rate two fat mallards are lying on the front porch and Otto is allowed to watch through the closest window while Uncle goes outside to get them. Otto mashes his hot moist face against the chilled glass and is quiet. They do not look like ducks to him, but that is what his father said; therefore they must be ducks.

Uncle stoops to catch each mallard by a foot. Already the birds are freezing to the step and when he pulls them up they resist; Otto sees that a few feathers remain on the cement. The front door opens for a second while Uncle comes in, each bird hanging by one foot so that its other yellow web seems to be waving good-by. The heads swing underneath. The male looks almost a yard long—it cannot be that big, of course, but Grimes and Uncle, who is still snuffling, agree it is the biggest mallard they have ever seen. Around its green neck is a lovely white band; Otto reaches out hesitantly to discover if it is real. The neck feathers are cool and soft. The female is a mottled brown and buff, a small one, not much more than half the length of the male. They are dead, this Otto knows, but he is not certain what death is, only that one must watch out for it.

John Grimes takes each bird around the middle and everyone is a little surprised when the heads rise, just as though they had finished feeding, but the reason is simple: the necks have frozen. Grimes holds both mallards up high; he cracks the cold orange beaks together and smiles down at Otto.

"Quack! Quack!" blurts Uncle.

Otto knows who made the noise and pointedly ignores Uncle, but he cannot get enough of staring at the refulgent bodies. He has never seen anything so green, or of such tender brown. The breasts are full and perfect; to find out what has killed them one must feel around in those feathers, parting them here and there with the fingertips, until the puncture is suddenly disclosed. Side by side are the two held up as if in flight, though the wings have stiffened forever.

Otto is subdued, and when the episode of the ducks is ended, when they have been taken roughly into the kitchen and nothing more can be said of them, he must struggle to regain his plaintive tone. Now there is not a chance it will be successful but he says he thinks Donna would like a drink. It is not successful. However, there are two big guns that Otto always keeps in reserve; one is that he believes he is getting a stomach ache and the other is that he is afraid the stars are falling. He is no fool, this Otto, and realizes that if he tries them both on the same evening he will be found out. He studies his bare feet like a politician and estimates which question would be most effective, considering the fact that there are some ducks in the house and that his mother has been in bed all day. He begins to look wonderfully ill at ease.

"Are the stars falling down?"

Always that is good for an answer, a long melodious one, always. But tonight it is met by a grim stare from his father. He looks hopefully at his mother; she is not so ominous but equally firm. There is about the atmosphere something that tells Otto he is about to get turned over his father's knee. He backs toward the stairway with hands behind him, wondering if he could reasonably ask for the dog-in-the-manger again. His father places both hands flat on the table, which means he is going to stand up. Otto abandons all hope, and, wearing a persecuted face, goes up the stairs as rapidly as possible, which is to say in the manner of a chimpanzee.

Almost immediately there is a crash in the upstairs hall followed by the unmistakable sound of Otto falling. Once

again he has forgotten about the hall table. Originally
there was a vase on this table but after he destroyed it
while hurrying to the bathroom they reasoned that sooner
or later he would take the same route; hence there is nothing but a lace doily on the table. In fact, Muhlbach finds it
a senseless place to put a table, but his wife wants it there
though she cannot explain why. Otto is bellowing. To listen to him one would be convinced that in all history no
individual has ever experienced such pain. He varies pitch,
rhyme, and tempo as he recalls the tragedy; it is a regular
Oriental concert. The footsteps of the nurse are heard, and
the mutter of her scientific soothing, but he will have none
of this professional.

Joyce gets up from the table, but in passing behind
Muhlbach's chair an expression of nausea overspreads her
face and she almost subsides to the floor but recovers without a sound. Kirk started to cry out, and upon seeing her
straighten up he emits a weird groan. Dee Borowski and
Muhlbach gaze at him very curiously.

Otto can still be heard, although the sincerity of his
dirge may now be questioned. At any rate he has been carried to bed, where the nurse tenderly swabs his bumped
forehead with mercurochrome and covers it with a fantas-
tic bandage that he seems to enjoy touching. Still he is so
exhausted by the hour, the splendor of the ducks, and the
strange men, and the accident in the mysterious hallway
that it is necessary to continue whimpering. This self-
indulgence halts the instant he becomes aware that his
father has entered the room. Otto prepares himself like
any rascal for he knows not what judgment, and cannot conceal his apprehension when his father draws up a chair
and sits wearily beside the bed. They talk for a while. Otto

does not know what they are talking about. Sometimes they
discuss his mother, sometimes himself, or Donna. He in-
dustriously maintains his end of the conversation though
he feels himself growing sleepy, and in time he is neither
displeased nor alarmed to feel the hand of his father strok-
ing his head. Somewhat groggily he inquires if the stars
are falling. In addition to being a useful question Otto is
moderately afraid of just such a catastrophe. He did not
come upon this idea second-hand, but thought of it himself. The first time it occurred to him he began to weep,
and though a number of months have gone by so that he
trusts the sky a little more he is still not altogether confident. One can not be sure when a star is falling. Clearly
there is nothing to hold them in place. Why should one not
suddenly drop on his bed?

Countless nights, in winter and spring, autumn and summer, have Otto and his father gone out of doors, or sometimes driven toward the country far enough that the city
lights were humbled, and here, with the boy on his father's
lap, they have considered what was above. At first there was
a certain difficulty in communication. For example, Muhlbach spoke on the constitution of stars while Otto listened
with profound concentration. Muhlbach was impressed
until Otto, after a period of meditation, inquired if Donna
was a star, a question that might be answered in various
ways, of course, depending. But with practice they began
to understand one another so that after several months
Otto grew familiar with the elementary legends and was
apt to request his favorites, such as Andromeda, or The
Twins. Or he might ask to hear that wonderfully eupho-
nious index to the Great Bear, which goes: Alkaid, Mizar,
Alioth, Megrez, Phecda, Merak, and Dubhe.

"What does the bear eat?" he asks, and this is certainly
a question packed with logic. His father's faith is renewed;
the lessons continue. Not far behind the bear—do you see?
—comes Arcturus, its warden, who follows the animal
about. This happens to be the father's personal favorite
among the stars because it was the first one he himself
ever learned to recognize, and was taught him by his own
father, the very same who gave young Otto the archaeology
book. Muhlbach hopes that Otto will learn Arcturus before any other. This is the reason he points to it first of all.
He directs the flashlight beam toward this yellow giant, so
many times larger than the sun, and though Muhlbach has
searched the heavens with a flashlight numberless times
he is yet amazed that his light appears to reach all the way.

We can never go there, Otto. It is too far. Muhlbach in-
cludes a few statistics and is again deluded by his son's intelligent expression because it develops that what Otto
wishes to know is whether or not Arcturus is farther away
than downtown. Still, hope springs eternal, and after
smoking half a cigar Muhlbach has recovered from the
blow enough to try again. Once upon a time—yes, this is
the right approach—once upon a time Arcturus came flying straight toward the earth! What do you think of that?
Otto is shaken by the premise; in his father's lap he sits
erect and anxious, no doubt pondering what will happen
when they meet, or met, since it is all in the past. Half-a-
million years, for that matter, and Muhlbach, now savor-
ing parenthood to the utmost, adds with a sportive air that
the sole observers were troglodytes. Otto lets this pass.
Now Muhlbach hesitates because he has pumped up his
story; the full truth is that Arcturus was also drifting a bit
to the side as it approached and even now is passing us so

there is not to be a collision after all. Fortunately Otto considers the telling of greater value than the tale. He is not much gripped by explanation or hypothesis; he would as soon just look. One would think he was gazing into a mountain lake. According to his father they can see perhaps three or four thousand stars in the sky; Otto again looks up and is stunned, though for a better reason. He is a pure voluptuary, a first-rate knight of the carpet. Sidereal time, relative motion, and years of light are all very well— astronomy, in short, can come or go, so Otto feels—but stars are magnificent. Briefly he is held by the constancy of Arcturus, then he loses it. There are a great many things in the sky. How shall he hold fast to one? When he is older he will distinguish more clearly but now a light is a light, each about as effective as its neighbor. Now he has been seduced by Mars. It seems bigger and more suggestive. What could he not accomplish if only he held it in his hand! As there is no moon, and Sirius is down, nothing can be more glamorous. How red it is! How wondrous bright! In vain does Muhlbach point out the planet's limitations.

In his bedroom the little boy sleeps with one arm raised and a fist clenched as if in triumph, on his helpless face a stubborn look, his forehead all but invisible under the preposterous mercurochrome-soaked bandage. Muhlbach sits beside his son, watching and thinking. The bedroom is silent but for the breathing of the two children. The nurse has gone downstairs. After a while Muhlbach rises and walks soberly across the room to stand above his daughter; her pink jade lips are parted and it is clear her dream is a serious one. Muhlbach wonders if she will sleep until spring. He longs to pick her up, somehow to unfold himself and conceal her deep within, and he bends down until their faces are an inch apart, but he keeps his hands clasped behind his back. Donna is oblivious to it all.

He hears the front door close, the faint after-knock of the brass lion's head on the outside of the door. He moves on tiptoe to the window and looks down at his two friends, the duck hunters, who elect to tramp across the snowy lawn even though the walk has been shoveled. He looks at his watch to discover he has been up here almost a half-hour. He very much wanted to go hunting this year, possibly more than ever before; each time this thought comes to him he feels unutterably disgusted with himself.

Uncle and Grimes leave dark symmetrical prints on the snow and as always Uncle is one step behind. There is no reason for this; it is just the way they are. It comes to Muhlbach that John Grimes is leading his afreet by a chain round the neck. He watches them get into Grimes' car, sees the headlights flash and thus notices that the snow has stopped falling, and moodily he looks after the burning red tail lights until the street is again deserted. That snowy rectangle over which they walked oddly resembles the eight of spades; and now the half-moon comes floating above the rooftops as if to join in this curious game. Much higher—well along in the night—kneels the father image, Orion. While Muhlbach stands at the window the moon's light descends calmly upon his troubled face and reaches beyond him into the nursery past Donna's crib to the wall poignantly desecrated by paste and crayon scribbles. There a swan is in flight. Otto has seen fit to improve this wall-paper swan. What could be gained by telling him its elegance is perhaps impaired by the measles he has added? Muhlbach thinks over the shards remaining from his own childhood, but is conscious mostly of how much has perished.

Some time longer he stands there steeping himself in this restorative moonlight, and looks around with approval at the knotty pine toy shelf he has knocked together and varnished, and again remarks the silence of this night which is counterpointed by the breath of his children. An unimpressive man he is, who shows a little paunch and the beginning of a stoop, though otherwise no older than forty warrants. People do not ever turn around to look at him on the street. At cocktail parties no feminine gaze lingers on him. When it comes to business there are men who find it worthwhile to seek out Muhlbach for an opinion; otherwise he is left alone.

Quietly but without disappointment he leaves the nursery, shuts the door, and descends the staircase hopeful that his wife has recognized the futility of this evening. It strikes him as incredible that she can maintain interest in a man she has outgrown.

When he enters the living room the nurse slips back upstairs. His wife and Sandy Kirk are making no attempt to communicate; they sit side by side on the sofa but behave like strangers seated together at a movie. Of course the presence of the dancer would forbid much action; however Joyce has never required much. Borowski appears hypnotized by the embers; she has taken off her shoes and placed them neatly like an offering on the marble hearth. Muhlbach finds her naïveté wearisome and he thinks that if she does anything else ingenuous he will just tell her to go home. But she does not even blink when he strides past; she does nothing but dully watch the subsiding flames, her mouth idiotically open. From his chair beside the bookcase he glowers at her, and it suddenly occurs to him that he is sick of the cook, too, and sick of the relentless nurse. He is sick to death of life itself, and of optimistic neighbors, and he has forgotten whatever is not despair. Too much is happening to him, whereas all he wants is to be left alone that he may regain some measure of his inner strength. Even one hour, uninterrupted, might be enough. He thinks he cannot pretend much longer. His thoughts turn upon Goethe, from whom he is remotely descended, and he visualizes that man interminably searching himself for power while playing to his sycophants a stiff-legged excellence.

Just then Muhlbach's wife shakes her head bitterly over some private thought, and looking at him she remarks, just loud enough to be heard, that John Grimes and Uncle left a few minutes ago.

Muhlbach discovers that his hands begin to shake with rage, so he allows himself a few seconds before replying quietly, "I know, I know."

Sandy Kirk rouses himself and places a hand delicately to his cheek as if he has just realized how suffocating the room has become. Muhlbach, watching Kirk, is filled with hatred; it seems to him that never before has he encountered a man he despises as much.

"They missed you," his wife continues, "but I told them you'd go hunting again next year—the same as before."

In this speech there is a note of self-pity that causes Muhlbach to shut his eyes and throw up his hands, though he does not say a word.

"I told them I was being selfish but I want you with me every minute of the time. Next year they'll have you the same as before." Having started she cannot stop; she turns swiftly upon Sandy Kirk and presses one of his limp hands to her breast. Her eyes fill with tears but aside from this she appears just peevish, and she talks to him steadily. Words pour from her nerveless mouth without meaning and Kirk is obviously terrified. He stares at her out of the corner of his eye like a trapped animal; he is powerless to recover his hand. Muhlbach scowls at Dee Borowski who has turned around to watch, and he knows that she is aware of him, but she cannot get enough of the nauseating scene; she must look and look. Muhlbach springs out of his chair and rushes into the kitchen.

Sandy Kirk turns his head this way and that to avoid looking at Joyce. All the precautions he took, they were no good. She has not respected any convention; she has lunged through every defense and taken him. Even under the circumstances it was not decent of her to do that. She has always shocked him one way or another, even the first time they met. He had been a college student then and one afternoon was standing on a snowy bluff overlooking a river that had frozen along the banks. He had brought along a sled and was wondering if he dared coast down because the slope was studded with pinnacles of rock; furthermore, if he could not stop at the river's edge there was a possibility of crashing through the ice and drowning. Then he noticed this girl trudging up with a sled. When he warned her it was unsafe she replied, "Mind your own business," and without hesitation flung herself upon the sled, hurtled down among the rocks, and reappeared far out upon the ice, wriggling to a stop not five yards from the water. That was the way she did everything. Now she is twenty-nine years old, a wasted old woman who can scarcely walk without assistance. Her arms have shriveled to the bone and the veins are black.

Kirk is furious that Borowski has not reacted the way she was supposed to. When at last he had gathered the will to speak, to interrupt the horrible monologue, and pointedly mentioned Don Juan, the dancer only looked at him in stupefaction. So he has not distracted Joyce, she has still got him by the hand, but he has located his voice, which has always been his ally, and it has begun telling something about something funny that once happened in Switzerland. Kirk waves his free arm and rolls his eyes comically toward the ceiling until at last, thank God, Muhlbach comes out of the kitchen. It is over. Joyce loosens her grip with a sob and he begins to pull his fingers away one at a time.

With an ingratiating tone Sandy Kirk addresses Muhlbach, who gives back a clinical stare and stretches out his hands to the fire. Seeing this calm gesture of self-assurance, seeing as it were, a true Hofmeister, Kirk suffers a familiar malaise, for among diplomats and intellectuals, or artists of any description, he feels established, but faced with a solid pedestrian he loses confidence in his own wit and commences to doubt the impression he is making. It has always been so, though for the life of him Sandy Kirk fails to understand why. And this Muhlbach is indestructible, a veritable storm cellar of a man. No catastrophe will ever uproot him or confuse him, this man of the flatlands with a compass on his forehead. Kirk is envious, and also contemptuous. He is a little afraid of Muhlbach. He has finally managed to get his arm more or less free of Joyce yet she clings mutely with her eyes. He feels sorry for her and wishes he could feel more, but there it is: she seems to him unreal and distorted, not the girl he once knew. This sick woman is distasteful. In the future he may feel more compassion but this evening she has driven him backward till he has begun to grow violent. If she does not soon release him altogether he will throw a fit. He cannot stand being forced this way, being accustomed to having what he wants only when he wants it. During intolerable situations Sandy Kirk always envisions himself in some favorite locale thousands of miles away. It is a form of ballast. And now he thinks he would like to be near Biarritz seated regally on the hillside on his favorite bench. From there he would contemplate the Atlantic sun shining on red tile rooftops, and after an expansive supper he might wander into the casino to luxuriate in the sound of clicking, rattling chips and the suave tones of the croupiers.

Otto has wakened; he can be heard talking to the nurse about something, no doubt vital. A jack-in-the-box will go down for the night more easily than will Otto. Recently he has taken to singing in the middle of the night; he disturbs everyone in the house with his pagan lament. "What are you singing about?" he will be asked, but he always refuses to answer.

Just then the telephone rings. Who could be calling at such an hour? Sandy Kirk, like a doctor, must always leave word of his whereabouts, and so does the dancer, though with more hope than expectation. As usual the actual message is less exciting than the suspense. Joyce, whose call it was, returns to the living room almost immediately. She seems more vexed than she has been all evening and after resting for a minute she mimics the inquisitive neighbor.

" 'I saw your lights were still on and simply thought I must find out if there was anything I could do.' She got a

couple of ducks, too. Your friends are dreadfully gener-
ous."

Muhlbach makes no attempt to reply. He shakes his head
as if he can endure nothing more.

Joyce Muhlbach's voice begins to rise unsteadily. "I told
her not to telephone this house ever again!"

Borowski has emerged from her private reverie long
enough to gobble this up and Muhlbach, who was watching her, is again filled with loathing. Little by little everyone in the room becomes aware that a group of carol singers is approaching, and finally, in passing the Muhlbach
home, their song is clear. The voices are young; most likely
a group of students.

After they have gone Joyce slowly resumes twisting her
wedding ring; it is loose on her finger and slides off easily,
hesitating only at the knuckles. She takes it off and puts
it on and all at once remarks that she has received an ad
from a mortuary. In this there is something so ghoulish
that it is almost impossible not to laugh. Her husband of
course knows about the advertisement but the guests have
a tense moment. Joyce glances from one to the other in a
malicious way, twisting her ring and sliding it off, waiting
to see if either of them dare smile.

Borowski becomes flustered. "Sandy has told me everything about you." This gets no response at all. Borowski
turns red, and says that Joyce meant a great deal to Sandy
years ago. Neither was that the proper speech so Borowski
glares at Sandy Kirk because it is his fault she has gotten
into this situation.

Joyce is suddenly aware that Donna has wakened, and
though not a sound comes from the upstairs nursery this
same knowledge reaches Muhlbach a second later. Both of

them wait. He glances across the room to her and she catches the look solidly as if she had been expecting it. Kirk guesses they have heard one of the children and he recalls that earlier instant when they reacted as a unit, causing him to sense how deeply they were married. He is a little injured that they mean this much to each other; he feels that Joyce has betrayed him. He knew her long before Muhlbach ever did. It is as if something valuable slipped through his fingers while he was preoccupied. Now he thinks that he intended to come back to Joyce. They would have gone well together, and he knows that whatever Muhlbach may have brought her he did not bring something she has always needed—excitement. Muhlbach took her by the hand and gently led her into a barren little room, a cool study where she has withered. Kirk feels himself growing embittered over the way life has treated him. This woman was rightfully his own, even if she refused to admit it. There were instances, it is true, when she became tyrannical, but later she would always repent; and if he should abuse her he had only to hang his head until her eye grew milder. To his mind comes the observation of one of those lugubrious Russians: that from the fearful medley of thoughts and impressions accumulated in man's brain from association with women, the memory, like a filter, retains no ideas, no clever sayings, no philosophy, nothing in fact but that extraordinary resignation to fate, that wonderful mercifulness, forgiveness of everything.

The longer Kirk sits in the room with Muhlbach's wife the more does he perceive how terribly he is still in love with her. He had been afraid this would happen. She is one of those legendary creatures whom the French have so astutely named *femme fatale*. One does not recover. Kirk has himself a furtive look at the husband. Yes, he has been stricken too.

What kind of a woman is she? One talks to her a little while of this or that, nothing remarkable is said, nothing in the least memorable, and one goes away. Then, all un-invited, comes a feeling of dreadful urgency and one must hurry back. Again nothing is said. She is not witty, nor is she beautiful; she is in fact frequently dour and sullen without cause. Periods of gloomy silence occur, yet no sense of emptiness, no uneasiness. She seems to wait for what is about to happen. It is all very confusing. Sandy Kirk broods, puzzles, gazes hopelessly into space for vast amounts of time thinking of nothing, unable to formulate questions worth asking himself, much less answer, feeling nothing at all but a kind of dull, unhealthy desire.

He steals another look at Muhlbach and discovers in that stolid face a similar misery, which makes Kirk feel better. He remembers with embarrassment certain tele-phone calls during which he was unable to speak. "Hello," he will mumble, already despondent at the thought that she is listening. "Is that you?" And when she replies, sounding stubborn, or irked that he has telephoned at such an inconvenient hour, then every single thought ex-plodes like a soap bubble. He waits anxiously to hear what she will say next, which is nothing: he is the one who has called, it is up to him to manufacture a little conversation. But he is destroyed by aphasia, he finds nothing humorous about life, not a thing worth repeating. What has he been doing? Well, quite a lot but now he thinks it over what is worth the effort of describing? He summons all his strength: "What have *you* been doing?" He has just man-aged to mutter this. She replies in an exhausted voice that she has not done anything worth mentioning. This is impossible! He mumbles something about the fact that he has been thinking of her and called to find out what she was doing—what a stupid thing to say, he realizes, and discovers to his amazement that he is clutching the telephone as if he were trying to strangle it. The wire has been silent for five minutes. He prays no operator has decided to investigate this odd business or he will be locked up for insanity, and in a voice more dead than alive he demands, "Are we going out tonight?" He is positive she will say no, and that is exactly what she does say. Instantly he is filled with alarm and wants to know why not; she replies callously that she doesn't want to see him ever again, but offers no explanation. He subsides. He leans against the wall with his eyes closed. He has not eaten all day but is not hungry. Minutes pass. Neither of them speaks. It is raining, of course; water splashes dismally on the window ledge and life is implacably gray. One cannot imagine sunshine, laughter, happiness. He staggers and understands that he was falling asleep. He whispers good-by and waits. She immediately answers good-by. Neither hangs up. Love is not supposed to be like this. He announces his good-by again with renewed vigor just as though he were rushing out to the golf course, but the mummery sickens him. There is no significant click at the other end of the line. What is she waiting for? Will she never release him? Can she possibly expect him to hang up first? Life is a wretched joke. He cannot abide the sound of his own name. Still she refuses to hang up the receiver, and it goes on and on, a long, dreary, stupid, inconclusive affair. These calls have on occasion lasted a full hour or more though neither of them said a good minute's worth. How desperate was the need to communicate, how impotent the message. So when he sees her he wants to know why she does not talk to him over the telephone, and she looks at him without a smile.

Kirk decides he is losing his mind. Has Muhlbach, that barn of a man, disgraced himself in a similar manner? Because normal men do not ignore their pride. Yet look at those tormented eyes! It is clear that he, too, has fallen apart in front of her. There could be no other explanation.

Kirk will never forget one night he went shambling through the streets without enough energy to lift his head until all at once, as though he had been handed a telegram, he started rapidly across the city, rushed through Times Square with his eye fastened on Forty-fourth Street, and just around the corner there she was! He was paralyzed that it had all come true. She was looking at him the instant he came around the corner, but she was holding to the arm of some nondescript man in a bow tie. As they passed each other he nodded curtly and stalked into the crowd. What a lover does he make! What happened to the celestial phrase? He is the sort of man who would address the wrong balcony. Even his agony is fraudulent because he is hoping everybody on the street notices his tragic face. He thinks he could not be more obvious with the stigmata; still, nobody paused when he strode somberly toward the river. Well, he has been through no grimmer night than that one. It might have made sense if she had been a famous beauty, but even in those days no one ever picked Joyce out of a group. She never was quick on her feet, or had a musical voice, nor did her skin ever take the light as the artists say.

At this instant the cook appears, not in her black uniform but in a rather shocking dress. She has finished every dish and emptied the garbage and now she would like permission to go home. Muhlbach calls a taxi for her. Cook bids good night to everyone, to everyone except the ballerina, and then she returns to the pantry where she will sit like a monument on her favorite stool to brood until the taxicab arrives. All have noticed her going upstairs a few minutes ago with a sweet for the children. She wakes them up to feed them something that will ruin their teeth; nothing can break her of this habit. Neither explanation nor threat of dismissal deter this cook, not even the formidable nurse. Cook is of the opinion the children are her own and it is clear that her heart would fall open like an overripe melon if Muhlbach ever made good his threat. The nurse and the cook look upon one another as hereditary enemies and neither questions that this should be so. Nurse dislikes going into the kitchen and while there is apt to sit with arms crossed and a severe expression. Cook feeds her without a word, stinting just a little, and afterward scrubs the dishes quite fiercely. She has never seen this nurse before; who can tell how reliable the creature is? Cook believes this nurse is neglecting the babies and thus it is she sneaks upstairs at least once a night. That is why, when Muhlbach calls for something, there may be silence in the kitchen.

All at once comes the sound of a shot. Conversation stops in the living room. There are no cars on the street, so it could not have been a backfire, and besides it sounded as though it were in the house. Muhlbach is about to investigate when at the head of the stairway appears the nurse, dreadfully embarrassed, to explain that she has been listening to a mystery on the radio, and has it tuned down low of course, but the climax, that is, the murder, was unnecessarily violent. She hopes they were not alarmed. She just now looked into the nursery; the children were not awakened. No, they are accustomed to sounds like that. Machine guns and bombs are natural toys nowadays.

Well, there it is; cook has not committed suicide after all. Presently the taxi may be heard crunching up the street. One expects it to climb the little drive, but it does not, even though Muhlbach has sprinkled rock salt from the street to the garage. Cook expertly flickers the porch lights but this taxi driver is leery of hillsides and does no more than blink his headlights by way of announcing that if she wishes a ride she must take the risk. That is the way of cab drivers nowadays; one must bow to their high-handed manner or simply do without. And should you fail to tip them they may slam the door on your fingers—cook often tells about the friend of a very good friend of hers who lost a thumb just that way and almost bled to death. Oh, it is a gruesome tale indeed and always concludes with the cook nodding darkly, hands folded severely over her white apron. She believes in a day of reckoning with as much faith as she attacks her Sunday hymns in the kitchen. These, by the way, have made her a neighborhood celebrity; whenever she is mentioned someone invariably adds, "—the one who sings in the kitchen." The cab driver, ignorant of the future, states his position by lighting a cigarette, and at this the cook capitulates. She lets herself out the screen door—so anomalous in winter—and is heard walking cautiously down the icy steps. One can see her getting into the back seat of the cab. The door is closed and she is taken away, unhappy woman.

The children—"my babies," she calls them—are undisturbed that she has left. They are never sure whether they dream of her nightly visit or whether they really do wake up and eat something. No matter, they will see her the following morning. Just before noon she will arrive, lumbering and scolding without even waiting to learn what they have done wrong. If they have been really bad she will frighten them by saying she is going to California. Their eyes open wide. It is the word alone that Donna has come to fear; the sound of it is enough to make her weep. Otto knows it is a place far off in the direction of downtown where people go when they are angry, and he knows that no one ever returns from California, so he too begins to sob. Oh, there is no punishment worse than when cook starts packing her suitcase.

But they are sleeping now. Otto is a little boy, there can be no question of that, but Donna, what is she? She is so small! Can anything so tiny be what she will one day be? Will there come a time when she would abandon her father and her brother for the sake of someone they have never seen? Someone perhaps as impossible as Otto, or even more so? Surely no one more obstinate and militantly ignorant than Otto can lay claim to being human. Only wait and see! He will come for Donna with biceps flexed and a hat crushed on the back of his head. Most likely he will be chewing gum. He will converse like a cretin, yet how accomplished will he think himself. Will Donna think as much? Will she peer into her mirror and suffer anguish over the shape of her chin or the cut of her gown? She could not be more perfect yet she will despise herself because of him. Perhaps he will even be tattooed! He is so clever and so handsome, she thinks, how can it be that her father pokes fun at him? Well, her father has grown old and does not know about the latest things. In fact Donna is mortified that he chooses to wear the kind of collar and necktie he does; it might have been very well in Mother's day, but that was twenty years ago. "How just positively incomparable!" she exclaims over his old-style collar, or about the latest motion picture. "How simply positively incomparable!" she cries at sight of her girl friend's new pair of dancing slippers. A month later everything has become "beautific." Her father mulls over the expense he has gone to in sending her to a decent university where she was to learn English. All in vain. She has learned her grammar from comedians. How lovely she is! Muhlbach feels tears surging to his eyes, but of course nothing shows. Why not? Why is he unable to weep for beauty that is positively incomparable? And he thinks of her mother, and when Donna twirls about the living room for him with flushed cheeks Muhlbach cannot trust himself to speak.

Who can say whether this will all come to pass? Is that the way it is to be, or will panic annihilate them all? Perhaps such horror will occur—bombs and irresistible rays not yet invented, a holocaust even the comic-books have not conceived—that Donna will never be stricken by this ludicrous young god. In view of the damage he is sure to inflict perhaps it would be well she died in the wreckage of a war. Well, they will all find out.

Now, this starry night, she lies serenely sleeping, a Botticellian morsel, the cook's beloved, an altogether improbable object, cherished above life itself.

Otto, being masculine, cannot afford to be so complacent as his sister, not even in dreams. His fists fly back and forth, he cracks his skull against the wall and does not feel a thing, he thrashes, mutters, climbs mountain peaks, vanquishes his enemies in a second, and above all else he frowns. Not for him the panacea of Donna's rag doll. A gun may be all right for a time, a puppy is even better, a picture book is good too, and attempting to climb the willow tree is a worthy project, but there seems to be no final answer. He must wrangle first one thing and then another, and in each he finds something lacking. Here he is scratching at the screen door again though he wanted to go outside not five minutes ago. His nature is as restless as the nose of a rabbit. No one can be certain what he is seeking.

He is wakened by something going on downstairs. The voices have changed somehow. There is the sound of coat hangers rattling and of people moving around. Company is going. Otto looks groggily at the ceiling and tries to stay awake though there is no profit involved. He would like to get up and look out the window but the room is cold; then too the nurse would probably come in and he does not especially like her. He has thought up some grisly tortures that he intends to try on the nurse, such as flooding the bathroom and when she runs in to turn off the water he will lock the door so that his father will think she did it. Otto has a great bag of schemes for the nurse. He is certain to drive her away. Meanwhile he must concentrate on the noises and so understand what they are doing downstairs. Donna is breathing passionately at the moment and Otto is annoyed by this interference; he props himself up on both elbows.

The front door opens and people can be heard going outside. This is really too much; Otto is wide awake and out of bed, creeping to the window. There he crouches, his brilliant eyes just above the sill. The winter air makes his eyes water so he grinds his fists into them, the best remedy ever. And he shivers without pause. He has come unbuttoned again.

Muhlbach is following the guests down the icy walk to Kirk's car. Its windshield is a mound of snow and while the guests are getting into the car Muhlbach reaches out and brushes off the windshield. This is no instinctive action: for the past hour he has been thinking about this gesture. When he opened the door for Grimes and Uncle he noticed the snow still falling and saw that it was about to cover the other car. Not long after that he hit upon the proper method to end the evening, a simple act not only cordial but final. It should express his attitude. Now he has done it but too fast; Kirk was not even looking.

The engine starts up. The diplomat has fitted on his elegant gray gloves, settling each finger, and now pulls the overcoat across his knees while waiting for the engine to warm. Beside him the dancer is already beginning to look snug; she has drawn her rather large strong feet up onto the seat and tucked her hands deep inside the mink sleeves of her jacket. She is only waiting for the instant the wheels begin to turn, then she will lean her head against his shoulder and like the wheels she will roll toward a conclusion. She is always touched by this moment when the acting is done, the curtain comes swaying down, and life takes over. Each time, however, she is a little frightened, a little doubtful that she can survive.

Muhlbach, standing soberly beside the hood, brushes more snow from the edge of the windshield and receives a faint shock when Kirk acknowledges this by glancing out at him; for an instant the man looked older, much different, the hair on his temples appeared silver. Muhlbach is well aware that Kirk is eight or ten years junior, yet he cannot escape the eerie feeling that he saw a man distinctly older than himself.

Throughout the evening these two have avoided each other, and so it is destined to end. Circumstances have set the limit of their association. They must be neutral forever. Sandy Kirk has divined the truth of this while Muhlbach was thinking it through. They nod. The car starts forward but immediately slips sideways into a rut where the wheels spin ineffectively. Kirk, tightening his grip, presses the gas pedal to the floor and Muhlbach realizes the man is a poor driver. The tires are screaming on the ice. Muhlbach throws up both hands, shakes his head, goes around to look, and sees that he must get out his own car to give Kirk a push. In a few minutes it is done; they are safely away from the curb.

The visitors have gone. Muhlbach eases his car once more into the garage and closes the door, but despite the extreme cold he cannot bring himself to return to the home right away. While he stands forlornly gazing down at his shadow on the moonlit snow he hears the voice of his son crying timorously into the windy night.

Muhlbach lifts up his head. "Go to sleep, Otto."

And the apprehensive Otto, peeping down from the nursery window, hears this faint reply. It is the voice of his father saying everything will be all right.

The Yellow Raft

From the direction of the Solomon Islands came a damaged Navy fighter, high in the air, but gliding steadily down upon the ocean. The broad paddle blades of the propeller revolved uselessly with a dull whirring noise, turned only by the wind. Far below, quite small but growing larger, raced the shadow of the descending fighter. Presently they were very close together, the aircraft and its shadow, but each time they seemed about to merge they broke apart—the long fuselage tilting farther backward, raising the cold heavy engine for another moment, while the shadow, like some distraught creature, leaped hastily through the whitecaps. Finally the engine plunged into a wave. The fuselage stood briefly erect, a strange blue buoy riddled by gunfire, and then, bubbling, inclining, it sank beneath the greasy water. A few seconds later, as if propelled by a spring, a small yellow raft hurtled to the surface with such violence that it almost took off. It wallowed back and forth, the sides lapped with oil. Suddenly a bloody human hand rose out of the ocean and clutched it. For a little while nothing else happened; the raft floated calmly over the swells and the man held on. Then he dragged himself into the raft and lay there crying bitterly. A few minutes later he was sitting up, cross-legged, balancing himself against the motion of the raft and squinting toward the southern horizon, for it was in that direction he had been flying and from that direction help would come. After staring at the horizon for about an hour he pulled off his helmet and began toying with the radio cord; then he lay down in the bottom of the raft and covered his face with his hands. Late that afternoon he again sat up and began to open the pouches along the inside walls of his raft. He found signal flares, first-aid equipment, some dehydrated rations, and a few luxuries, and when the sun went down he had just finished eating some candy and was lighting a cigarette. He blew a few smoke rings in defiance of the sea, however a west wind developed and before long he stopped mocking his host; he zipped up his green coveralls to the neck and turned up the collar against the spray. Next he tightened the straps and drawstrings of his life jacket and lay down once more, bracing his hands and feet against the sides. He was sick at his stomach and his wounds were bleeding again. Stars appeared all around the raft. Several hours passed in total silence, except for the slosh of water and the occasional squeak of rubber as the raft bent over the crest of a wave. Spume broke lightly but persistently on the man huddling with his back to the wind. Suddenly a rocket whistled up from the raft and illuminated the scene. No sooner had its light died away than another rocket burst, and then another, and another, and another until there were no more. But there was no answer. Overhead wheeled the Southern Cross, Corvus, Hydra, and Libra. Before dawn the lost pilot was crouching on hands and knees, peering intently toward the southern horizon. Presently he thought he saw a marine reptile as large as a whale, but with a long swanlike neck, pass underneath the raft and emerge from the water some distance away, and as he looked into the depths the pilot discovered that the sea was filled with living things. The water bulged all around and from everywhere bloomed the fiery tentacles of the sun. Occasionally, on a crest, the pilot was drenched with spray. Then he waited with a remote stare as the raft, with a sickening, twisting slide, sank into the trough where the ocean and the ragged scud seemed about to close over it. A flashlight on the bottom of the raft rolled to one side, hesitated, and came rolling rapidly back, while a deepening puddle of sea water appeared now at the pilot's feet and now at his head and sometimes submerged the flashlight. The rubber walls of the raft were slippery, and the pouches from which he had taken the rockets and the cigarettes were now brimming with water. The drawstrings of his life jacket slapped wildly back and forth. He had put on his canvas helmet again, and a pair of thin leather gloves to protect himself from the sting of the spray. Stubby, foaming waves rose abruptly, without rhythm, to sweep over the walls of the raft, and left the pilot covered with salty bubbles. The ocean and the sky had fused; he could not tell whether he was vertical or horizontal, and he no longer cared. By noon he was drifting through a steady rain, his eyes closed. Whenever the raft slipped into a trough the final vestige of light disappeared; then, with a splash and the squeak of taut rubber, it spun up the side of the next wave, met the onrushing crest, and whirled down again into darkness. In the middle of that afternoon a layer of dingy phosphorescent light disjoined the sea from the sky; then the

waves grew massive and took on a solid greenish-black
hue, like volcanic glass, each vast undersurface curved and
scratched as if by the grinding of pebbles. The pilot waited
and watched as one colossal wave after another dove under
the bounding yellow raft. When the storm had passed it
was night again and the constellations were overhead as
before.

At dawn, from the south, came a Catalina flying boat,
a plump and graceless creation known as the PBY—phleg-
matic in the air, more at home resting its deep snowy
breast in the water. It approached, high and slow, and almost flew beyond the raft. But finally the tremendous wing
of the PBY inclined slightly toward a yellow dot on the
ocean, and in a stately spiral the flying boat descended,
keeping the raft always within its orbit. Several minutes
later, a few yards above the water, the PBY skimmed by
the raft. Except for the flashlight rolling idly back and forth
and glittering in the sunshine, the yellow raft was empty.
The PBY climbed a few hundred feet, and, after turning,
crossed over the raft again. Then it climbed a little more
and began to circle the raft. All morning long the Catalina circled, holding its breast high like a great blue heron
in flight, the gun barrels, propellers, and plexiglass blisters
reflecting the tropical sun. For a while at the beginning of
the search it flew tightly around the raft, low enough to
touch the water in a few seconds, but later on it climbed
to an altitude from which the raft looked like a toy on a
pond. There was nothing else in sight. The only shadow
on the sea was that of the Navy flying boat moving in slow,
monotonous circles around and around the deserted rubber raft. At one time the PBY angled upward nearly a mile,

its twin engines buzzing like flies in a vacant room, but after a few minutes it came spiraling down to continue as before, the inner wing pointing so steadily at the gaudy raft that the two objects might have been connected by a wire. The horizon remained empty. On the tranquil, sunny ocean no spars or crushed debris were floating, nothing to mark the place where the fighter had gone down, just the raft which was smeared with oil and flecked with salt foam. Early that afternoon a blister slid open near the tail of the Catalina, and a moment later a cluster of empty beer cans fell like little bombs in a smooth glittering trajectory toward the sea, splashed, and began filling with water. A few waxed sandwich papers came fluttering down and floated on the ocean some distance ahead of the sinking beer cans. All through the long afternoon nothing else happened, except that once again the water seemed to grow restless, and a thin veil materialized in the sky, diminishing the light of the sun and deadening the rich color of the Coral Sea. Well before dark the Catalina turned inward, carefully, till it pointed straight at the raft. Then for the first time in many hours the insignia on its prow—a belligerent little duck with a bomb and a pair of binoculars—rode vertically over the waves. The prow of the Catalina dropped as it approached the raft, and the tenor of its engines began to rise. The huge flying boat descended with ponderous dignity, as a dowager might stoop to retrieve a lost glove, and with a low, hoarse scream it passed directly over the raft. An instant later, inside the blue-black hull, a long thin gun began to rattle. The raft bounced on the water until the gunfire ceased. The strange dance ended. The yellow raft fell back, torn into fragments of cork and loose, deflated rubber. From these remains came floating an iridescent dye, as green as a rainbow. The Catalina, its work complete, began to rise. Higher and higher in the air, never changing course, it flew majestically toward the infinite horizon, leaving the darkness and the silence.